MW01132685

As We Lay Dying

Amy Clarkson MD

This is a work of fiction. Names, characters, places, and incidents either are the product of the author's imagination or are used fictiously. Any resemblance to actual persons living or dead, events, or locales is entirely coincidental.

Copyright © 2020 by Amy Clarkson MD

All rights reserved. No part of this book may be reproduced or used in any manner without written permission of the copyright owner except for the use of quotations in a book review.

Cover design by Amy Clarkson MD
www.amylclarkson.com

Printed in the United States of America
First Printing: January 2020

ISBN 978-1-0924-8762-7 (paperback)

To all who have been privileged to
work with those at the end of life

TABLE OF CONTENTS

I. WASHED AWAY

Gail

Gail looped two plastic grocery bags through her knobby fingers, and with her other hand reached for the gallon of milk in the back of her SUV. Gripping the milk tightly, she attempted to reach up and push the button that would mechanically shut the tailgate. She strained against the weight of the gallon of milk and her shaking hand was almost to the button, when the milk seemed to leap from her grip. As it tumbled downward, the plastic container hit the rear bumper, and the trajectory changed towards Gail. Had she been healthy, she would have easily dodged the projectile. However, weakened from rounds of chemotherapy, and depleted by the cancer that grew inside her, she was unable to move fast enough. The jug made impact at her lower legs, shifting her balance backwards. All at once, she was sprawled on the cement driveway. In a twist of fate, a loaf of bread in one of the bags cushioned her head from splitting on the cement.

"You fool," Gail spoke to her 67-year-old self, "can't even go grocery shopping without getting hurt." She sat up as quickly as her body would allow, and her eyes darted to her house, praying her daughter inside didn't see the mishap.

As she heaved herself to a standing position she trembled. Despite the outward angry bravado at herself, she was fearful, sensing yet another task she would have to give up. Her breast cancer had already demanded so much, and yet it continued to strip away her independence.

Steady once more, Gail reached for the bags and milk. She was so absorbed in her thoughts that she didn't notice the trail of rose red drops she left as she walked through the cluttered garage into her home.

"Mother!" The garage door swung open and the exasperated tone of Gail's eldest daughter, Janice echoed. "You cannot just leave this house without telling someone!" Janice had inherited her father's build and was tall and stocky. She had streaks of gray in her short hair and never wore make-up. Janice stood towering over Gail with a hand on her hip.

"Can you imagine how terrified I was when I woke up and couldn't find you?" Janice's eyes changed from fury to panic as she narrowed in on Gail's left hand. "Mother! Good God, you are bleeding! What happened?"

Gail followed her daughters gaze and seeing the gash on her left hand, had the sensation of being a child caught with a stolen cookie. Janice gave her mother no time for explanations and ushered her into the house, scolding her continuously as she grabbed a dishcloth for the bleeding.

The groceries forgotten, Janice evaluated the gash. She was

a high school science teacher, and was not squeamish around blood, but she quickly could see this was beyond her scope.

"I'm going to call Tami, your hospice nurse. This is pretty deep." Janice caught Gail's gaze and saw the shame and defeat written on her face.

"Oh Mom, I'm sorry. I'm sure it was an accident, but really! You are acting like nothing has changed, trying to do everything on your own. You have cancer! You must let us help, so things like this don't happen."

Gail nodded sheepishly. She knew there was truth in her daughter's words, but she just didn't want to accept that things had changed. Taking the dishcloth, Gail walked to the kitchen table to sit down. Her body announced that it was exhausted with each feeble step.

The late summer morning sunlight splashed onto the oak table, having just peaked over the evergreens lining their backyard. She became lost in her thoughts, remembering the summer they moved into this home, 30 years ago. It was a new home, with a newly sodded yard, and a few planted sticks that were meant to be trees. Her husband, Dean, had insisted they plant a row of evergreens for privacy. Gail smiled recalling how she had sat as she sat now, looking out the window. Janice, 13 at the time, had been clearly in charge, shouting commands and directing her siblings. Sharon, age 10, had spent more time finding the right outfit for the project, than helping dig. Then there was Nathan, sweet Nathan, 8 years of age and over eager to please his father. Nathan had been Dean's shadow. It was the only summer they were all together. By the next year she and Dean were divorced, and Gail had quickly learned to do everything herself.

Janice's voice interrupted her thoughts, "Tami will be here in about 30 minutes. She said we need to keep pressure on it while we wait." Gail shook her head in assent but did not turn from her view. Soon she heard Janice on the phone again talking animatedly with Sharon. Inwardly she sighed, knowing this small thing would stir everyone into a frenzy.

Gail was aware nurse Tami meant well, but even she was in the category of 'them'. Gail felt she was in a standoff with the rest of the world. 'They' were the hospice nurses, doctors, family, and friends, who continually pushed her to do less, take it easy, or let others pick up the slack.

As expected, when Tami did stop by to clean and dress the gash, she sided with Janice.

"I'm sure it's hard to give up your independence," Tami spoke gently, kneeling by Gail's side, "but this injury is a reminder that serious consequences await you if you don't let your family help!"

Janice and Tami stood in the entry way and spoke quietly about Gail. Gail couldn't hear their words exactly, but her skin prickled with anger. Wasn't this her house? Wasn't this her life? Why then, did it feel like she was becoming a prisoner?

Gail heard the door close, and as Janice walked towards her with an uncomfortable look on her face, she prepared herself for the verdict.

"Mom, Tami and I were just talking." Janice absentmindedly began to pop her knuckles. "I know I was due to head back to Topeka tomorrow and give you a break, but we really feel you shouldn't be alone."

"Janice…," Gail spoke up in protest, but Janice held her hand up, stopping her mid-sentence.

"No, Mom, don't argue. Sharon thought the same thing when I talked to her earlier. We are going to split our time up, and make sure you are safe."

"But…," Gail tried again to speak up. She was feeling a rush of panic and claustrophobia.

"I'm sorry," Janice cut her off, "this is our final decision. We love you too much to let something happen to you." Janice turned and walked from the room, signifying that the conversation was over.

✱✱✱

Six weeks had passed, and Gail still struggled to do as much as she could on her own. She was down to 80 pounds and avoided mirrors at all costs. She felt like the same woman inside, but she'd reach for her cup of coffee in the morning and get startled at the twig-like-arm that held the mug. Someone has replaced my arm, she'd think. It didn't matter how many times this happened, it always took her a moment to reconnect to the ravaged body that was now her own.

"Mama," Sharon called sweetly from across the kitchen, "can I get you some eggs?" Sharon also was an educator like Janice. She taught middle school choir and tended to hum much of the day. She was thin and petite like Gail and wore her long hair in a bun most days, always tied with eccentric scarves.

Gail cleared her throat and tried to speak up; her voice didn't seem to have power behind it these days.

"No, I'm not hungry."

Sharon frowned but didn't hound her mother. Gail appreciated this about Sharon. Janice wouldn't have let up until Gail had consented and eaten one bite.

Gail glanced at the clock on the wall. 8:42 A.M. Eighteen more minutes. She would never admit it to her kids but sitting up in a chair was painful and exhausting. The most comfortable spot for her was her hospital bed. And yet, she forced herself into a chair once a day, for thirty minutes. She had convinced herself that the strain and hardship was staving off further deterioration. Today the minutes were molasses, moving abnormally slow.

Sharon sat down next to Gail with her plate of scrambled eggs. The smell nauseated Gail, but she didn't want to complain, so she plastered a smile on her face instead.

"You know Janice comes today to take over for me," Sharon stared at her eggs, moving them around mindlessly with her fork. "Well, the thing is, before I take off, Janice wants me to help her give you a shower." Sharon hesitatingly glanced in Gail's direction.

Color drained from Gail's face, and she began shaking her head 'no' before her feeble voice said, "No."

Sharon bit her lower lip, fighting the urge to give in to her mother's refusal. "Look, I know you want to do your own shower, but it's been ten days since you've been strong enough to stand on your own." Sharon paused briefly, "You need a shower. I'm sorry, but Mom, you smell."

At this Gail closed her eyes, unsure if she was more threatened by the idea of having her daughters help her shower, or the shame of not realizing she was dirty.

After her husband, Dean, had left, Gail had become a bit of a socialite. She organized parties for her book club, helped plan galas for local non-profits, and had earned the reputation of someone who was reliable and meticulous. When she had been asked to sit on the board for the Kansas City YMCA, her friends swarmed to her house to celebrate. Gail quickly threw together snacks and decorations using the theme from Village People's "YMCA" song. Her friends had been blown away by the coordinated spur of the moment event, and still talked of how amazing she was. Gail had to admit, even when her friends teased her about her constant immaculate appearance, she relished it as a compliment.

"Do you sleep with make-up on?" They would mock. "Do you even own sweatpants?" Pride welled within her with each faux jab.

Thank God they couldn't see her now, she thought. She was mortified at the idea that she hadn't even realized she had a stench. This, she reminded herself, was precisely why she was allowing no visitors.

"Mom? Are you alright?"

Gail had forgotten her eyes were still closed. More often, she found it easier to stay in her mind. She knew in her core she didn't have the strength to fight her daughters on the shower idea, so she opened her eyes and heaved a surrendered, "Fine."

✶✶✶

Gail was dozing in her hospital bed when she felt a hand on her ankle. She opened her eyes and saw Sharon standing above her with an encouraging smile on her face. Gail matched the grin, and then heard Janice's commanding voice on her other side, "Ok, Mother, time to do this shower so Sharon can get on the road."

Gail's grin faded immediately, and she felt the pangs of anxiety begin to boil in her abdomen.

"It's okay, Mama. We are going to be gentle and quick. We'll have you spruced up in no time." Sharon attempted to reassure her mother.

They got her up and transferred into the wheelchair with little effort. The master bedroom had ample room to maneuver around since they'd taken down Gail's king-sized bed and replaced it with the hospital bed. The master bath had a large shower and shower chair that hospice had provided.

As Janice pushed her the seven feet into the bathroom, Gail shivered, despite her thick sweatshirt and pants. She felt like a middle school girl getting ready to take her first communal shower in the locker room; shy and embarrassed. Gail's arms were locked across her chest in a protective way. She knew logically there was nothing to hide; her breasts had been removed in surgery 2 years ago. However, the habit was engrained. Years before she was diagnosed, she had watched the cancer grow. At first a small sore on her left breast, it slowly opened and enlarged. It would drain at times and even bleed. It kept getting larger, but Gail had not wanted to mention it to anyone. She would stand in public with her arms crossed, self-conscious that people could tell what she hid under her bra.

When the ulceration grew larger than a golf ball, she finally decided to go see a Doctor. Nathan and the girls had been livid with her for hiding it from everyone for so many years. At the time, the thought of letting someone see the growth was more painful than the risk that it was something ominous.

Janice turned on the shower and steam began filling the room, obscuring the mirror. Sharon laid towels on the edge of the shower, since the door would need to be open for them to help.

"Time to get your clothes off," Janice announced. Gail was used to dressing herself, however, over the last 3 days it had been too hard to change clothes, and she wasn't about to ask for help. It was definitely time for the oversized gray sweatshirt and pants to be replaced.

Janice stepped closer to help Sharon, "Okay, let's get this top off first." Gail reflexively tightened her arms around her chest, bowed her head and shut her eyes.

Sharon knelt in front of her mom and placed her hands on Gail's upper arms. She spoke softly, "Mama, it's going to be alright. Please let us help you."

Gail relaxed slightly, which was the sign Sharon needed to proceed. She gingerly unclasped Gail's arms and straightened them, then nodded to Janice. Janice worked on pulling the back of the sweatshirt over Gail's head as Sharon pulled off the sleeves. Gail couldn't help re-clasping her arms as soon as the shirt was off.

Sharon continued, "Janice is going to reach under your arms to help you stand so I can get your pants off."

Gail flinched at the touch of Janice's arms, firm and muscular, under her arm pits, lifting her to stand.

After the pants and underwear were off, Gail pivoted to the shower chair and Janice helped her to sit, water streaming down Gail's backside and drenching Janice's arms and shoulders.

It was only when the chore of getting Gail situated was over, that both girls took in the sight before them. Janice and Sharon's eyes locked, both communicating their shared horror through their looks.

Gail wasn't just thin, but skeletal; her bones and joints clearly visual underneath the sagging skin. Large purple and red bruises and sores littered her legs and arms and trunk. There was a smell that clung to Gail, as if something had soured and spoiled in the sun.

Sharon soaped up a washcloth and began softly scrubbing Gail's back and arms. Janice took charge of washing Gail's hair, working shampoo into her scalp.

Gail was hunched up as much as possible, trying to become nothing, and still closing her eyes. She raised her hands to cover her face and began to weep as the girls washed her.

Sharon heard the quiet sobs and her heart ached. This was too much, Sharon thought. She finished washing abruptly and turned to get an extra-large towel. Sharon nudged Janice, who was just rinsing out the shampoo, and said sternly, "That's enough. We need to be done."

Janice looked confused but turned the water off. Sharon wrapped the large towel around her mother, who shielded her face, still feeling shamed. Sharon couldn't keep her emotions at bay, and leaned into her mother, crying as she said, "I'm so sorry, so sorry, Mama."

Two weeks passed, and Gail now needed help with every aspect of living. The new schedule always had two of the siblings at the house to help with the cares. Nathan, a Physical Education teacher at an elementary school three hours away, had started coming every weekend. He was the baby of the family, and the girls were a little jealous at the effort Gail made to stay awake and talk when Nathan was there.

Hospice came three times a week, and took care of the more intimate tasks, though it was still a struggle. Gail resisted bed baths even with the hospice caregivers, Tami and Ruth.

On this particular morning, Janice had left to run errands and Nathan had chair duty. Gail slept more than she was awake, yet when she did awaken, she would panic if someone wasn't sitting by her bed. Nathan sat in an armchair nearby, watching ESPN's SportsCenter on his mother's television.

He became slowly aware that his mother was rousing. She was lying on her side, and her legs began to draw up and then down under the thin sheet covering her. Nathan turned his attention to Gail, lowering his upper body to be more in line with her vision.

"Morning, Mom."

She opened her eyes, and recognizing Nathan, she smiled. Just as quickly, though, a look of concern spread across her brow, and she let out an uncomfortable moan. Nathan noticed then that she was shivering.

"Are you cold? Hurting? What's wrong?" Nathan rose to find a blanket and Gail whimpered again, closing her eyes in discomfort. He grabbed a plush down comforter draped over another chair in the room.

He was just getting ready to encase his mother, when she tried to protest with a grunt.

"Mother, what's wrong?" Nathan was confused and concerned. Gail's legs moved again, restlessly. Nathan reached out to still his mother's legs and felt dampness through the sheet. A zing of connection surged in Nathan's brain.

"Oh, that's the problem." Nathan couldn't bring himself to say the words. "It's okay. I just need to get you out of those wet clothes and sheets."

"Please, not you," Gail managed to spit out, through chattering teeth.

Nathan took on the role of stern parent, "Sorry, I'm all you've got. This is just something we are going to have to get through." He tried to sound confident, but inwardly he was nervous. He walked out to the hall linen closet, and saw his hands trembling as he reached for a new set of sheets. Pull it together, he thought to himself, you have no choice.

He snatched a new gown from the dresser on his way back to the hospital bed and placed the clean items on the chair he had been sitting in. He decided not to look at his mother again and went to the side of the bed that her back faced. Nathan was thankful he had listened when the hospice nurse had trained them on how to change sheets.

He took the top sheet that loosely covered her off and threw it on the ground, as a waft of pungent urine filled the air. Next, he took the corners of the fitted sheet off and log rolled the sheet and thick pee pad towards Gail's back. He placed the new fitted sheet on the bed and another clean pad he rolled half way open. The hard part was next.

"Mom, I'm going to take your gown off now."

Tami from hospice had shown them how to take Gail's regular night gowns, and cut an opening up the back, allowing the gowns to slip on and off with little effort. Staying at her backside, Nathan pulled the wet gown through Gail's top arm. He paused for a moment, unable to look away from Gail's skeletal back. He would have expected to see her spine and vertebrae but was shocked to see each and every rib showing. On her tail bone, he saw a large red ulcer like a crater oozing something foul. Tears welled in his eyes and he came around the front to finish his task.

As weak as she was, Gail sobbed through her chattering teeth.

"It's time to roll to the other side." Nathan worked hard to gain control of his emotions, but it was hard to ignore his mother's discomfort. He helped her roll to her back, then her opposite side. She clutched her arms around her chest in an attempt to remain modest.

He pulled the log rolled dirty sheets from under her and off the bed, then reached for the clean set under her and worked and smoothed them onto the mattress. Every time the top of his hands grazed his mother's skin, she visibly cringed. He took the other arm out of her wet gown and tossed it away, putting her

into the new clean gown. As he rolled her back again to the original side to put the final sleeve in place, his tears spilled freely. He
cried, not just at the effects the cancer had taken on his mother's
body, but for the shame she felt as her dignity ebbed.

The final top sheet he tucked into the end of the bed and drew
up to his mother's shoulders, her hands now cupping her face,
shielding her from Nathan. Nathan knew nothing would make
things better, so he simply placed a hand on top of his mother's
head and kissed her temple.

✳✳✳

Days passed and soon it became too hard to be at home, and
a move to the Hospice House ensued. Janice paced the room
and glanced again at the non-descript clock hanging on the
wall. 9:25 A.M. Nathan was stretched out on the hospice room's
couch, sleeping soundly. Sharon, who sat in a chair next to her
mother's bed, watched Janice and remarked, "The nurse said she
guessed the Doctor would be in here between nine and ten. You
need to calm down."

Gail had been transported at 7 A.M. to Kansas City Hospice
House after a tense night in the home. She had called out, "Help
me," incessantly. Despite days of such profound weakness, that
she couldn't even swallow water, that night she had attempted to
sit up and escape her hospital bed. All three grown children, as
well as Tami their nurse, had fought the restlessness and finally
made plans for a transfer.

"It's just like going to the car mechanic," Janice grumbled,
"Mom's going to be nice and peaceful when the Doctor shows
up."

Sharon was too exhausted herself to want to expend energy sparring with Janice. It was true that their mother now seemed to be soundly asleep, but isn't that what they wanted? She tried to switch topics, "Did you see that funny man walking down the hall when we got here?"

"What?" Janice asked as she stopped pacing.

"You know, that old man that looked straight out of the 70's, wearing a winter cap and carrying a violin!"

Janice smirked at Sharon, "I think someone needs to get some sleep before they start seeing leprechauns and fairies as well."

At that moment there was a knock on the door. Amazingly, Nathan who had been able to drown out the girl's conversation, bolted upright at the knocking sound, rubbing his eyes and trying to appear awake.

Dr. Audrey Clark walked in, smiling and quickly taking in the room. Audrey was thirty-something, and exuded confidence mixed with warmth. She always tried to greet the patient or most senior person first, as a means of respect. She went to Janice and introduced herself, then around the room to the other two, ending up at the head of Gail's bed, across from Sharon.

Audrey gestured for Janice to take a seat, as she herself sat down.

"Tami, your nurse, told me what a rough night you all had," acknowledging the legitimacy of being there relaxed Janice immediately.

Audrey continued, "What your mom experienced last night is something we call terminal restlessness."

The word terminal sent a shiver up Sharon's spine, and she hoped for clarification and asked, "Which means what exactly?" She saw in Nathan and Janice's eyes that she wasn't the only one concerned.

"It's a phenomenon that most people go through when they transition to active dying. It must be a hard sensation to experience; our soul's trying to separate from our physical beings. Most of us fight against it and become restless. We don't know why, but we want to escape; our clothes, our beds, ourselves."

Janice tried to integrate this information into her mother's behavior last night and found it workable.

"She's so peaceful now. I mean, she hasn't been this out of it for three days. What does that mean?" Janice asked.

Audrey adjusted her tone. It was never easy to talk about death. "Her peacefulness, I think, means her transition is through." Audrey paused to give time for their minds to catch up and then concluded, "It means she is actively dying."

Stillness settled. A few tears spilled from Sharon's eyes, but no one spoke.

Nathan cleared his throat, interrupting the heavy silence, and sheepishly asked, "How much time, do you think?"

Audrey nodded her head, looked at something written on a paper in her hand, and then rose and lifted the bed sheet to look at Gail's feet. Gail's feet were a bright purple, causing Janice to gasp.

"Is this new?" Audrey asked, touching the ice-cold purple feet. All three looked shocked and nodded.

"This is called mottling. It's not painful, but is a result of poor circulation, as the heart slows on it's way to shutting down. The mottling, her low blood pressure, the fact that her kidneys aren't working, and her profound unresponsiveness, make me think she has less than 24 hours."

The siblings spent the next minutes talking with Audrey about symptoms and things to expect. As Audrey stood ready to leave the room she said, "I know I said 24 hours or less, but seeing even how she's had some subtle changes while I've been in the room, it could be any time now."

✷✷✷

At 1:15 P.M. Audrey was informed that Gail had passed away. She hated short admissions, as there was not enough time to connect to people. Gail was only at the Hospice House six hours. She made her way back down to room 16 to give condolences to Gail's children.

Inside the room, she patted shoulders and sympathized with them. She moved to step out and Sharon followed, asking for a minute of her time.

"Dr. Clark, this might seem strange, but what's the process now?"

"Not a strange question at all, the nurses will clean her up, and then, when you all give the okay, the nurse will call the funeral home. We are on no time table, so take as long as you need."

"Actually, here is the strange question. Can my sister and I be the ones to clean and bathe our mother?" Sharon blushed and bit her lip.

Audrey gazed at the ceiling, unsure what to say. Finally answering, "I don't see why not. I'll let the nurse know."

Sharon reached for Audrey's hand as her eyes filled, "Thank you." Audrey walked off trying to surmise what that was all about.

✷✷✷

The nurse, Victoria, had set out everything the girls needed. A plastic basin was filled with warm soapy water, and several wash clothes and towels were folded nearby. Victoria had explained that they usually put on a new gown and gave a bed bath but didn't wash the hair. Before Victoria left, she took both girls' hands in hers, and told them she thought what they were doing was very meaningful.

Unlike the shower the girls had given their mother at home, Sharon took the lead for this one. She dipped a washcloth in the warm water, wrung it and handed it to Janice. She felt like a priest handing out the sacrament, Janice's hands open to receive the blessing. Janice moved quietly to one side of Gail, and Sharon prepared her own washcloth. As if in a ritual, Janice waited for Sharon to take her place across the body. Their eyes locked for just a moment, and all the words they would never be able to say passed between them.

Sharon took the top sheet and walked it down and off the bed. Both girls took their free hands and pulled the gown from their mother's shoulders, down her rigid body, and off the bed. Clearly lifeless, pale and gray like a plastic doll, it was still mom. They both half-expected her to squirm and raise her arms in protest. There she lay, completely exposed, the mastectomy scars cutting across her flat emaciated chest.

They began at her forehead and worked to her feet. They never spoke. Tears mixed with soap and water as they cleansed her, their gentle strokes were their words, and their final touch was their goodbye.

2. UNFINISHED BUSINESS

Chelsea

Chelsea's heart pounded inside her chest and she felt the all too familiar wash of dread drench her like a bucket of ice water. She was already propped upright in her bed, her husband, Jared, snoring next to her. She saw the neon red lights of her clock across the room; 2:07 A.M. Why must I always wake at two, she wondered, while simultaneously trying to ignore the panic intruding into every cell of her body. Who was she kidding, she couldn't fight this fear. The very thought of being consumed by terror gave more power to the anxiety and her breathing quickened. Was her throat closing? She couldn't get enough air.

"Jared!" She cried out, "Help, please, I can't do this!"

Jared instinctively sat up. His eyes half open and not quite awake, "Huh? Chels? What's going on?"

"I can't breathe, something's wrong!" Chelsea's slight frame rocked forward and back, her hands clenched on her side. Her wide-open dark brown eyes were in such sharp contrast to her pale skin and bald head that she looked like an owl perched in their bed.

Jared was fully awake now and he moved so his muscular frame enveloped her into his side, trying to stop her rocking. "Shhh, now, it's okay. I'll get you another Ativan."

"It's not going to work this time," Chelsea whimpered, "I'm dying."

"Chels, remember what the Hospice nurse said, this is a panic attack. Your brain is tricking you. C'mon, the Ativan will work, I promise."

Jared slid his right arm down to grip her hand as he turned the rest of his body to reach for the light on his side of the bed. His commanding confidence already began to ease Chelsea's spinning mind. He peered at the plastic bin on his nightstand which functioned as a mini pharmacy. There were prescription bottles, lip balm, lotion, over-the-counter cough drops, and lemon candy. At 34, he knew far more about the medical world than he had ever wanted to know.

He didn't unclasp Chelsea's hand until he needed it to undo the safety lock on the orange see-through pill bottle. "Do you still have water in your glass?"

Chelsea nodded, her expression still pained. She reached for her water and took the chalky pill from Jared's outstretched hand and swallowed it. Only then did she turn to look at her husband of 8 years. "I can't do this," she whispered.

Jared felt something acidic rise into his throat. He didn't

know what to say. He had gotten pretty good at being her nurse. When Chelsea was diagnosed last year with cervical cancer, he jumped in fully. His landscaping business had ample employees to fill in the gaps when he took Chelsea to chemotherapy and follow up appointments. Chelsea's parents took over much of the house work and stepped in to be in charge of their two sons, JT and Max. They were a team playing tug of rope with cancer. They strained and pulled, dug in their feet and cheered each other on. Two weeks ago, the rope had been yanked out of their hands. There were no more treatments to offer. The sudden loss of the tension caught them off guard. They found themselves stumbling and falling, unsure of what to do.

Without any words to answer his wife, he squeezed her hand and encouraged her to try and rest.

✶✶✶

It was Dr. Audrey Clark's first day back to work at the Hospice House. She felt a sense of coming home after her turn working at the hospital doing consults. She thought briefly of Albert, her last hospital consult, a curmudgeon of a man she'd discharged home from the hospital the day before. She wondered if his estranged daughter would be able to handle his personality and their tumultuous history.

Despite the safety and comfort she had working at the Hospice House, she still felt a small seed of angst walking in to her shared office space. The first day back presented the challenge of meeting all new patients and trying to establish a connection.

Dr. Annabelle Calando, the senior partner, had called Audrey the night before to verbally hand off the patients she was passing on to Audrey.

"The toughest case is the woman in room 14," Annabelle had cautioned. "She is 32 with metastatic cervical cancer. Two children ages 2 and 7. She has been in for a week with intractable vomiting and pain. I have her on intravenous dosing intermittently, but she'll probably need that adjusted."

"Sounds like an existential crisis," Audrey had surmised.

"Most likely it is, thus the challenge."

Audrey knew she wanted to start her morning in room 14 to try and unearth if the woman's symptoms were coming from a physical source, or in fact, were due to suffering, that intangible powerful force that was grueling to treat.

On her way down the hallway, Audrey was energized by the welcome backs she heard from staff. Many wanted to know how her 2-year-old daughter, Izzy, was doing. She pulled out her phone and showed off the latest photo of Izzy, face painted purple and cheeks puffed out as if blowing a balloon. Victoria, a 40 something experienced hospice nurse laughed heartily at the face paint, and added, "You know Max looks a lot like Izzy, minus the purple."

"Max?" Audrey was confused.

"Chelsea's son, Max, you know the patient in room 14? He's two as well and seems as ornery as Izzy."

Audrey felt a tightening in her chest and put her phone away. "Oh right! I was just going to go meet her."

Victoria filled Audrey in on medications used and gave Audrey her own insights into the hard to control symptoms.

It wasn't until Audrey was in Chelsea's room, however, that the realization sunk in that they were both the same age. Chelsea was sitting up in the hospital bed, a bright red knit stocking cap hiding her bald scalp. She looked to be dozing, a pink plastic basin next to her side, and a handmade blue and yellow quilt covered her legs. Her wrinkle free skin sagged slightly from weight loss, and yet it was clear she was a beautiful woman. On her left a muscular and olive-skinned man, whom Audrey guessed was her husband, slumbered in an arm chair. To Chelsea's right, a woman who appeared to be an older version of Chelsea, slept with her armchair reclined fully. The rest of the room was littered with cards, balloons and flowers. There were toy trucks and kid's books in piles. Photos of their carefree times of the past littered the mantle of the faux fireplace in the room.

The man stirred first and wiped the matter out of his eyes, "You must be the new Doctor that Dr. Calando told us about. I'm Jared." His tone was warm and matter of fact. Perhaps recognizing Jared's voice, Chelsea roused, an immediate frown folding itself across her face. As she came to consciousness and opened her eyes, she abruptly reached for the basin and bent forward over it. Jared came to her aide, and Chelsea's mom woke at that commotion.

Chelsea's shoulders heaved and her stomach attempted to empty, but nothing came out. Audrey stood awkwardly, waiting for the moment to pass. Both Jared and Chelsea's mom were clearly used to this, as they each filled a particular role without speaking. Jared helped hold the basin and placed his other hand on Chelsea's shoulder and spoke calmly. The mother went into the bathroom to retrieve a wet wash cloth to cool Chelsea's face and nape of her neck.

The episode passed and Chelsea glanced up at Audrey. There was such a look of pleading in her eyes that Audrey almost gasped audibly but held herself steady.

"I should at least introduce myself, I'm Dr. Audrey Clark." They all gave perfunctory nods. "Let's talk about this vomiting and how we can do better." Audrey approached and took a seat gingerly at the foot of the bed. "Can you think of anything that triggers the vomiting?"

Chelsea shrugged her shoulders in a defeated way. Jared piped in, "It seems to happen whenever she wakes up."

"Have you noticed if any medicine works better?" Audrey inclusively glanced at all three of them.

"Nothing," Chelsea quipped.

"I think the Ativan does the best." Chelsea's mom said, adding protectively, "I'm Ruth by the way, Chelsea's mother."

Audrey smiled at Ruth and then turned to Jared, "Do you think the Ativan helps?"

"Yes, it's just that it knocks her out. Then she wakes up nauseated. We seem to always be chasing our tails."

Chelsea grimaced and leaned forward, whining, "Please, make it stop!" Her body repeated the previous movements, dry heaving again.

"Let me grab Victoria to give you a dose now. But I think I have an idea on how we can help this."

"Anything… please." Ruth's own voice had a gut-wrenching ache to it, the effect lighting a fire of determination in Audrey's core as she left the room.

Audrey waited until Victoria got back from dosing Chelsea to explain the plan to the seasoned nurse. "I know we usually use our I.V. pumps for pain medication, but I think we should try a continual infusion of Ativan for Chelsea. My hunch is having a constant low dose in her system will lower the angst she is feeling and yet not completely knock her out."

"It's worth a try," Victoria consented.

★★★

The day slipped by more quickly than usual. It was nearly four o'clock before Audrey was able to check in on Chelsea again. Audrey was surprised to find Chelsea alone in the room.

Chelsea opened her eyes lazily as Audrey asked, "Where is everyone?"

"Jared is running the boys back to my folks for dinner. He and my mom will be back after their supper." Chelsea's voice was parched, but more energetic than this morning. "Hopefully my dad will be able to handle their baths. Jared makes fun of me for always checking in on their hygiene." Chelsea grinned, "What can you expect? I am a hygienist, aren't I? Even if it is dental, it's all the same!"

Audrey chuckled, thinking of Izzy and how little she got bathed these days. She was tempted to start a dialog like most moms fall into, telling stories and comparing parenting styles. She squelched it, and made her way to the bedside, wanting instead to capitalize on their privacy. "Can you tell any difference with the Ativan now running constantly?"

The corners of Chelsea's mouth turned upward in a brief smile. "Yes, a big difference. I feel a bit detached, but I haven't had to vomit in hours." A flicker of pain crossed her brow and she asked, "How long though will this last? Even at home, something would work and then after a day or so I'd need more."

"I don't know how long this dose will work, but let me tell you something," Audrey leaned forward as if she was going to share a secret and placed her hand on Chelsea's lower leg, "there is always more to give. We will never reach a limit. There is no such thing as a ceiling when it comes to treating pain and anxiety."

The slight smile returned briefly, but then a tear formed in Chelsea's eye. "I just don't want to die."

Audrey was expending much energy, trying to keep a barrier up from experiencing Chelsea's feelings personally. She shook her head sympathetically, "I can't even begin to imagine all of the emotions you must be dealing with." Chelsea's tears came freely but she kept herself composed. Audrey decided to press a bit and asked, "What is the hardest part about this whole process?"

Chelsea turned to look at the mantle with the photos on them and focused on a large picture of a sandy haired boy missing two front teeth, his hands on top of a toddler's head, who stood in front of his brother with a big pot belly and toothy grin.

"I'll tell you what the hardest thing is: Not knowing which is worse, having a seven-year-old who will remember me and miss me when I'm gone, or having a two-year-old who will grow up with no memories of me and therefore won't miss me at all."

The image of Izzy's purple face burst into Audrey's mind and sadness welled up like a volcano ready to explode. She physically clenched her jaw to force the image away and focused back on Chelsea. But what could she say to this young mother, faced with an unimaginable question of what was worse?

When Chelsea looked back towards Audrey, her expression looked like the one Audrey had seen that morning. Anguish flooded her features and she looked like she'd be sick again. Her eyes rolled to the back and her muscles tightened, she moaned, "Here we go again."

Audrey reached for the basin and mimicked what she'd seen Jared do, putting her hand on Chelsea's back as Chelsea attempted to expel her grief and pain into the pan.

Over the next 7 days, Chelsea's medications were adjusted

daily to keep on top of her symptoms. Chelsea slept more often and more deeply. Initially this bothered Jared and Ruth, but Audrey tried to help them understand what it must be like to be Chelsea, awake and flooded with powerful feelings of sadness, fear, and regrets.

Audrey's daily visits became times of storytelling by Chelsea's family.

"You should have seen how Jared asked Chelsea out the first time," Ruth's eyes sparkled as she told Audrey the tale. "She was a dental hygienist and Jared had been one of her clients. He had flirted with her and tried to get her number, but she had been through a bad break up and was adamant to not start dating again."

Jared sat across the room with a pleased expression on his face and jumped in, "I wasn't going to take no for an answer. I scheduled another appointment for a cleaning just two weeks later with her."

Ruth started chuckling, "This is so great, listen to what he did."

"I found this stage makeup for black tooth coloring, you know for Halloween stuff." Audrey nodded, still unsure where this was going.

"So I had my buddy spell out 'D. A. T. E. ?' on my front teeth." Jared was laughing now along with Ruth. "And I had him write it upside down, you know, so she could read it."

Audrey giggled, "Well what happened? What did she do?"

Jared finished, "She was already annoyed to see me again so soon. I had a hard time talking, trying to keep my lips covering my teeth until I was in the chair. When I opened my mouth finally, she let out a little scream." Jared's face filled with pride, "My creativity paid off. After she rolled her eyes and tried to pretend she was upset that I was ruining my teeth, she agreed to go out with me."

Audrey looked over at Chelsea who slept soundly, feeling the happy memory float down and settle onto her frail body. The room quieted as all of them focused on Chelsea.

"Why is it taking so long?" Jared feebly asked, adding, "I don't want her to go, but she hasn't eaten in two weeks, and at this point she is just lying there."

Ruth chimed in, "It's so hard for us to sit and watch this. I feel terrible saying this, but in some ways, I want her to go, to be done with this suffering."

Audrey nodded in agreement and said, "At this stage, it's usually the families who do the most suffering." Audrey held up her hands which she balled into fists and rubbed her knuckles together as she stated, "You both have two conflicting parts of your selves warring against each other. One part doesn't want her to die because you love her so much, and the other part wants her to die, so she won't suffer, again all because you love her so much."

Jared inserted, "I feel so guilty when I realize that I've secretly wanted her to die."

"Exactly!" Audrey confirmed, "It's extremely difficult to harbor such competing human emotions simultaneously. Go…don't go. Of course, you'd feel guilty. But I wish you wouldn't. It's out of love, and frankly this battle is universal, I see it every day here."

"Really?" Ruth asked, a bit of relief in her voice.

"Absolutely. In fact, I'm sure Chelsea is going through the same battle within herself as well. It's probably one reason she's lingering here."

"Oh, I didn't think of that," Ruth said. She leaned over to Chelsea who was on her side, red knit cap still covering her head. Her cheeks were sunken, and her mouth rested in an open position. Ruth's lips hovered just over Chelsea's ear and she spoke in a quiet voice. "Sweet girl, don't hang on for us. Of course, we don't want you to go, but this is too hard." Tears spilled down Ruth's face and she half prayed, "Please. It's okay. You can go."

Audrey didn't want to invade the intimate moment any longer and excused herself, finding it hard to keep her own emotions stuffed inwardly. What she hadn't shared with them, is that she harbored the same struggle, many mornings hoping for the news that Chelsea had died while she was away.

It was Audrey's Saturday to be on call and she pulled into the parking lot at the Hospice House with a slight amount of discontent. Izzy and her husband promised they wouldn't have too much fun at home without her.

When she got her updated patient list, her gaze went straight to room 14 as it did every morning, to see if Chelsea's name was still written as its occupant. Day 17 without nutrition of any kind, day three of absolutely no response. The Ativan infusion still ran, but Chelsea hadn't needed any extra doses for those three days. Audrey was running out of things to say to the family. At this point they were all just waiting on Chelsea to let go.

Making her way down the hallway, Audrey saw a blur of movement, and realized it was Victoria skirting out of Chelsea's room. Her first thought was, maybe this is finally it.

She paused outside of room 14, waiting for Victoria to return, trying to listen for any sounds that would clue her into what was happening.

Victoria appeared, pushing a wheelchair, which completely baffled Audrey.

"Why do you need a wheelchair for Chelsea's room? Did someone visiting collapse?"

"Dr. Clark, you won't believe it. Chelsea woke up this morning, about 30 minutes ago. She's speaking a bit to her family." Audrey's eyes widened at this unexpected news.

She followed Victoria into the room, still unsure why the wheelchair was needed. Chelsea was positioned in a sitting posture in her hospital bed. At first glance, Audrey had a hard time believing she really was awake. Her eyes were closed, mouth still hung slightly open as she took slow deep breaths. Seeing her upright accentuated her gaunt appearance. Audrey felt that the slightest breeze would knock her back down into bed.

Hovering near Chelsea were Ruth and Jared, both looking excited and a bit frenzied. In the corner, Bill, Chelsea's father, sat holding Max on his lap. Max's eyes were glued to the television set where a muted cartoon aired. JT, the older boy, had his knees on the couch looking out the window, his chin rested on his crossed arms which were on the back of the couch. He appeared bored.

Victoria was in command moving the wheelchair into place and locking the wheels. She gave instructions to Jared and Ruth as they helped slide Chelsea to the edge of the bed and got ready to hoist her into the chair.

The movement stirred Chelsea and her eyes opened, though they had a glassy appearance and didn't seem to focus on anything. Her voice was hard to understand, but Audrey made out the words, "I need to do this. I need to...."

Everyone else in the room seemed privy to the plan, so Audrey just stood in the background as a witness.

Chelsea let out a slight moan when they moved her to the wheelchair. They then used pillows on either side to prop her in place, as her trunk strength was gone. Audrey was amazed to see Chelsea's eyes suddenly clear and a look of determination etched itself into her malnourished features.

"Okay, Max. You first." Chelsea's voice transformed to the commanding timbre of a mother and the toddler quickly hopped from his grandfather's lap and toward his mother. Jared intercepted him before he dove into Chelsea's lap.

"Whoa, buddy. Mom's fragile, let me help you up." Jared lifted Max and sat him gingerly on Chelsea's lap, his back nestled into his mother's slight frame.

Audrey couldn't stop her eyes welling with tears and noticed none of the other adults had control of their emotions either.

Chelsea had managed to pull from an unknown strength inside her, which now operated her previously immobile body. She wrapped one arm around Max's left side and dropped her chin over his right shoulder, fitting her cheek next to his. She then opened her palm to receive something from Ruth.

"Oh right, sorry." Ruth said mesmerized at the scene before her. Ruth had been holding an object in her hand, and gently laid it in Chelsea's outstretched hand.

Audrey turned to try and see and only caught sight of a glint of metal. It wasn't until Chelsea's left hand held Max's hand firm, flattening out his fingers, that she understood that Chelsea was going to trim his fingernails.

"I need to do this one last time, little man."

Audrey instinctively whipped her body around as her hand flew to her mouth, attempting to silence the cry that had bellowed up. This was too much, and Audrey silently let herself out of the room.

Chelsea preformed the ritual deftly, speaking softly to Max things only he could hear. A few tears fell from her face, which caused Max to turn his face towards hers and ask, "Mommy, why you cry?"

"Because I love you so much," Chelsea said, kissing him on the forehead and working hard to control her own tears. Jared sensed this intuitively and told Max he was done, and he should give Mommy a hug and let JT have his turn.

JT had been taking this all in, an understanding of what was to come engraved in the way his eye brows crinkled across his forehead.

When Chelsea called for him, JT was hesitant, battling his desire to run into his mother's arms with the unpleasant sight and smell of her.

He made his way to her cautiously, and Jared again helped in placing him on her lap. Chelsea went through the same actions as she had with Max, and JT visibly relaxed with the familiar ritual. Unlike his younger brother, when Chelsea had finished the final nail on his pinkie finger, he turned readily, twisting his torso and wrapping his arms around his mother's neck.

With her task completed, Chelsea quickly began to sink into herself again. In the short span of JT getting down and making sure the wheelchair was in the right position, Chelsea's lids had closed. Victoria and Jared, who just 20 minutes prior had hoisted Chelsea into the chair, found it hard to reconcile the limp worn out body they now tried to maneuver back into bed.

"I don't understand," Ruth questioned, her face blotchy and swollen from all the tears she'd shed, "Why is she so unresponsive now?"

Victoria finished tucking a sheet up under her arms and turned to the family. Their confused expressions implied they likely were all questioning the reality of what they had just witnessed with the listless shell before them.

"It's called a rally; a last surge of energy. It's fairly common for people to have one right before…" Victoria hesitated and glanced at the two boys, "…before the end."

Victoria added, "But, usually not this profound. Most of the time it's just someone waking up to say goodbye or squeeze a hand. This, this was a real gift." Victoria's own eyes were moist. Her eyes roved the room in a final assessment, making sure they had what they needed before she exited.

Victoria turned once more towards the family when she was in the threshold of the door, she wanted to thank them for letting her be a part of that moment, but looking at the boys, and seeing Jared huddled over his wife, and Ruth stroking Chelsea's brow, the words got choked in her throat. Instead, she left without words and carried her heartbreak and gratitude with her.

3. LOST

George

Tami glanced at her watch before she got out of her car. 11 A.M., she was over an hour late. Her head was still swimming from the harrowing morning she'd had. What was meant to be a 30-minute check-in with an ALS patient, turned into an emergency admit to the Hospice House.

I'm getting too old for this, Tami thought, as she grabbed her large nurse's bag and headed into Bright Creek Nursing Home. At the age of 52, Tami knew that she had at least a decade more of work ahead of her before she could even consider retiring.

Her canvas bag, chock full of adult diapers, wipes, gloves, and medical equipment, seemed to cut into her shoulder more today than ever, reminding her she needed to call her chiropractor for an appointment.

Inside Bright Creek, Tami did a quick scan of the open dining area looking for her patient. One elderly woman sat in a wheelchair at a table, head slumped over and dozing. Another woman with purple gray hair and a walker caught Tami's eye and made a beeline for her. Tami knew most of the residents from her frequent visits.

"Hi, Ethel," Tami smiled.

Reaching Tami, Ethel began with her usual topic of discussion, "Do you know when the bus is coming to take me home?" Ethel had been asking everyone she met this question for as long as Tami had known her.

"Sure don't." Tami didn't have time today to engage Ethel in a long dialog about the bus and turned to go.

"Wait, I need to know when the bus is coming. I don't want to miss it!" Ethel's tone was frantic, but Tami was forced to ignore it and make her way down the hall to her patient's room.

She reached room 114 without any further delays. The wooden door was shut, and a bright colored metal sun with the words "welcome" hung on the door. To the right of the door hung two 5 x 7 photos of the two men sharing this room. She looked at the photo of her patient, George Reynolds, 88 years of age, slender face, too many sun spots to count, kind eyes, and a slight grin. The photo of the roommate, Jack, reminded Tami of a Shar-Pei, as he weighed three times as much as George, and had layer upon layer of extra skin folds.

Inside the room, George had the bed nearest to the door. He sat next to the hospital bed, in an oversized wheelchair facing a small television set propped near the door on a small stand. Although George faced the set, on which a non-descript western aired, his eyes looked blank and uninterested. Tami took a few steps into the room and glanced around the flimsy curtain which separated the two roommates and noted that Jack was not in the room. She then flipped the television off and watched for signs of disappointment in George's facial features. Besides a blink, there was no change.

George was a new dementia resident to Bright Creek, and to Hospice. His daughter, Rebecca, had been caring for him in her home for the last year. Before that, George had lived with his wife, Reba. The dementia had started over a decade ago, but Reba had managed to adapt to the subtle changes over the years. A year ago, Reba had broken her hip, and then died of a sudden blood clot two weeks after her hip surgery. George became unhinged after Reba passed. Unable to cook, or dress himself, Rebecca had moved him into a spare room at her house. Rebecca took early retirement at 64 as a loan officer at a bank and devoted herself to her father. He was the only family member left. Her only brother Geoffrey had died in a swimming accident when he was eight years of age.

George continued to deteriorate, despite Rebecca's intense care. She fed him, clothed him, and bathed him. His speech was difficult to understand at times, and yet she patiently sat by his side hours of the day, listening and trying to connect to the man she had always known.

One frightening night, she had awoken to a chilling breeze. She bolted out of bed and to George's room down the hall. The light was on, the bed empty. She half ran to the kitchen, trying to keep her fears in check. A red glow emanating from the stove top caught her eye, and a skillet sat empty nearby reflecting the eerie hue of the heat. A rush of air rustled her hair, and she turned to see the back screen door open. "Dad," she screamed, unable to stop the bilious panic from erupting. Rebecca sprinted out to the back patio, allowing her eyes to adjust to the darkness, and she scanned the yard frantically.

Her brain registered a whitish figure in the far back corner of her yard, where her flower garden was. She ran towards the shape, not sensing the cool dew that coated her feet as she called for her father.

Relief flooded her as she neared, knowing it was him, and that he didn't appear harmed. He sat in one of the two metal chairs in the garden, his bare knobby feet poking out of his flannel pajama bottoms. He was hunched forward, white undershirt on, and one hand rubbing his mouth and chin back and forth in thought.

"Dad! What are you doing?" Rebecca's voice was still alarmed from the adrenaline pumping through her body.

George didn't look up or acknowledge Rebecca but did move his hand away from his chin. Rebecca thought she heard him murmuring, "eggs."

At that moment, Rebecca remembered the stove was still on, and told her father to not move as she ran back to the house, praying a fire hadn't started with her absent mindedness.

The event had shaken Rebecca's confidence as a caretaker. She stubbornly had thought she could do this on her own, but her mind flooded with other horrific outcomes that could have happened that night.

Days later George moved into Bright Creek and based on how quickly he was losing weight and losing skills, the facility had initiated hospice.

This was only Tami's second visit with George, and she spent the next 30 minutes assessing and examining George, trying to get him to interact. She spoke constantly to him, trying different subjects to see if anything caused a spark in his eye.

She was just finishing her visit when the door opened and a

spry middle-aged woman sporting short bobbed gray hair entered. The woman immediately approached George and kissed him on the forehead before kneeling to his side. Her face radiated love and she greeted him cheerfully, "Hello, Dad, it's about time for lunch."

Tami caught the twinkle in George's eye and made her presence known with a cough.

Rebecca turned, startled. "Oh, I didn't even see you! Sorry! I'm Rebecca Reynolds. You're not one of the nurses that works here, are you?"

Tami introduced herself as being with hospice, mentioning they had spoken on the phone the day before, and Rebecca nodded with a smile, but not before a flash of uncertainty crossed her face.

"Well, I'm here for a lunch date with this handsome man." Rebecca patted George's arm and he gave a little smile. "I have to make sure he gets a good meal. They are so busy around here, I'm worried if I don't feed him, he won't get fed."

"Just so you know, I can do that as well. Part of my job is to watch out for that very thing. That is, if it's a priority for you." Tami had quickly ascertained on the phone yesterday that Rebecca had a lot of misconceptions about hospice. One of the big things Rebecca believed was that hospice starved people. Tami was eager to dispel that myth.

Rebecca cocked her head to the side, "I didn't realize you would do that. So, if I can't be here, you will make sure he eats? It can take a while to get it all down"

Tami smiled; she'd taken care of dozens of patients with dementia and knew the slow patience it often took to feed someone.

Rebecca stood and offered an arm to her father, "We'd better get down there to get our seat!"

Tami watched George, who wasn't sure what to do. He reached up and took Rebecca's hand but didn't make an effort to stand. Rebecca was undeterred and changed her position so she could pull her father's body up with her clasped hand. She strained against his weight and encouraged him through gritted teeth.

"You know we could just take him down in the wheelchair," Tami interjected cautiously.

With a snort, Rebecca pulled harder and huffed out, "No ma'am, we have to keep his strength up or he will lose his ability to walk."

Tami swallowed back her opinion and instinctively went to help, displaying the proper technique. As she stood in front of George, she used her knees to block his and wrapped her arms around his waist. Rebecca let go of the arm she was yanking. Tami rocked him forward and then gave him instruction, "Lean forward George, and use those arms to push up. Ready, one, two, and three..."

George stood, and beamed, he glanced at his daughter. "Reba, let's dance."

Rebecca frowned, "Dad, it's me, Rebecca. Mama's not here." George's face sagged in disappointment and he looked confused. Rebecca took his arm, "Let's go have lunch."

Tami watched George shuffle out with Rebecca, and noted he was unsteady on his feet, but still able to walk.

With Rebecca taking care of lunch, she decided to check in with the Director of Nursing. The halls were now littered with residents on their way to eat. Some sat in wheelchairs, using their feet to slowly propel their chairs like toddlers in a Little Tike car. Still others hovered over walkers like mountain climbers, lunging their metal frames ahead into position, and then hoisting their bodies and legs to catch up. No matter the method, they all seemed trapped in a world whose tempo had slowed, on their way to an equally protracted dining experience.

The Director of Nursing's office door was open, and Tami peered in, glad to see the D.O.N., Fran, at her desk. "Knock, knock," Tami verbally drew Fran away from her computer screen.

"Hi, Tami, you must be here to see our new guy, George." Fran had been the D.O.N. for two years, which was a record amount of time for this nursing home.

"Just wanted to see if there were any issues."

Fran paused to search her thoughts, "Let's see. Did you bring any Boost supplements? With the 20 pounds he lost at home this last month, we wanted to add in the extra calories."

Tami shook her head no and made note of the need to drop the cans by tomorrow.

Fran added, "Our nurse last night, David, said George did wander a bit. I assume that is because he's still adjusting to this new location. I'll let you know how tonight goes, see if we need any medication."

"I'll check in tomorrow when I bring by the supplies." Tami hoped they wouldn't need more medication; she had a hunch Rebecca may not like the idea of sedating her father.

On her way out, Tami paused to observe George and Rebecca at one of the square dining tables. She watched George's eyes wander and get distracted at various things in the room. Rebecca would patiently redirect him and remind him to open his mouth to take the next bite that she'd swept up. Even once the bite was in his mouth, he needed reminding to chew. Like a cow working on cud, minutes seemed to pass, and then Tami saw George's Adam's apple move up then down, indicating he'd swallowed the bite. A small cough after the bite told Tami what she needed to know; he was aspirating when he ate. She grabbed her notebook from her bag and added reminders and information to include in her computer note later that night.

She turned to exit the building and found Ethel by the door, "Can you give me a ride? I think I missed my bus to take me home." Ethel's look was pleading and distressed.

Tami patted her shoulder as she entered the code to disarm and unlock the door, "Not this time, Ethel, sorry."

∗∗∗

When Tami pulled into the parking lot at Bright Creek the following morning, she was hoping to be in and out quickly. She had two cases of Boost to drop off, which she hoped would last a while.

Her plan for a fast visit seemed to be working, and even Ethel hadn't stopped to engage her today. Tami had dropped off the drinks, peeked in and saw George was sleeping soundly, and was just passing Fran's office when she heard her name being called. Internally she sighed and turned towards the voice.

"Tami, I'm glad I caught you. Will you step into my office for a minute?" Fran had a look of concern written in the lines of her face, and Tami's heart sank. What now, she wondered.

Inside the office, Fran shut the door and motioned for Tami to sit across the desk from her. Mentally, Tami began to run through her visit with George and Rebecca yesterday, wondering if she'd done or said something wrong.

Fran leaned over her desk and appeared serious. "We had a rough night with George last night." She paused, her fingertips coming together to form a triangle, "Frankly, we are a little…"

She searched for the right word, "concerned."

Tami was drawn forward by Fran's grave manner, and asked, "What happened?"

"I told you how David said George had wandered a bit his first night here, right?" Tami nodded recalling the statement. Fran continued, "I guess David saw George lean forward and kiss one of the photos outside a resident's door, but didn't think much of it, until last night."

In the silence, Tami tried to guess what Fran was going to say and feared the worst.

"Last night David found him up wandering and before intervening watched him for a while. Tami, he was walking up to each door and kissing each and every picture of the residents." Fran screwed up her nose in disgust. "David said it was creepy."

Tami let the image settle on her and could understand the repugnant factor.

Before Tami could speak, Fran shared her worry, "We can't let this behavior go on. If any of the residents saw this, or other family members, we could have real trouble on our hands." Fran paused and then added, "Take for instance, Louise, she screams for the police when any of the male residents say hello to her. She'd go ballistic if she saw her picture being kissed."

"Has he shown any aggressive or overt sexual behavior at other times?" Tami was having trouble reconciling the sweet, quiet man she met yesterday with the behavior that was being suggested.

"Nothing whatsoever, however, we need to act quickly. I'll let you coordinate between his doctor and family." Fran then added, "You know if he does act out, we will be forced to send him to a behavioral unit."

Tami cringed, "I understand. Let's see what we can do on our end and hope it doesn't come to that." Tami contemplated giving the Hospice Medical Director, Dr. Clark, a call to see what her thoughts were, but talked herself out of it, deciding she'd wait until medications were needed before bothering her.

In a split-second decision, Tami decided she'd go make one or two patient visits in the area first, and make it back to catch Rebecca for a face to face discussion after George's lunch.

✶✶✶

Tami walked briskly back inside Bright Creek praying she hadn't missed Rebecca. She scanned the dining hall and places residents congregated as she scurried down the hall to George's room. When she heard Rebecca's conversational voice near the door she relaxed, only to re-stiffen as she remembered the tough topic they needed to discuss.

Inside the room Tami greeted George and Rebecca and made small talk about lunch and the weather turning cool that morning. Tami knew she was stalling, and finally had the courage to ask, "Rebecca, would you mind if we spoke briefly outside the room?"

Rebecca's expression clouded with skepticism and she looked at her father, scanning him for something she might have missed. Not finding any changes, she hesitatingly rose and followed Tami out the door.

Rebecca crossed her arms defiantly and waited for Tami to speak. Tami absentmindedly rubbed the hem of her floral patterned scrub top, trying to decide how to start.

"Did anyone mention what happened…," Tami stopped mid question and started a different way, "Have you ever noticed any unusual behavior in your father?"

Rebecca was feeling defensive, "Unusual? As in not recognizing me, or thinking this is 1979, or assuming he's at work at the
bank today? It's all unusual."

Tami was struggling. "No, I mean, like unusual sexual activity?" Tami felt her face flush.

"Excuse me?" Rebecca's eyes looked like they would explode
out of her eye sockets, "What kind of question is that?"

"Sorry, I'm not going about this the right way," Tami's hand
had come up protectively, "Can we try to start over?"

"My father is one of the most honorable men I know." Rebecca didn't want to start over; she wanted this to be clear. "He
was married to my mother for 65 years! He doted on her, took
her dancing on weekends, and surprised her with flowers for no
reason. He was the kind of man that when others were being
vulgar about women, he'd get on them for being disrespectful."
Rebecca's eyes brimmed with tears as she continued, "For you to
insinuate some…," she searched for the word, "perverted behavior!" She couldn't continue and just shook her head in disbelief.

Tami's tone was soft and gentle when she answered. "I cannot
tell you how sorry I am to have been insensitive."

Rebecca softened, "It's just this disease. It makes me crazy.
You and everyone here, you don't know the man he was." Rebecca allowed the tears to come, "Actually, the man he still is, you
just have to look hard to find him in there."

Tami reached out to console Rebecca, and Rebecca allowed
herself to sink into Tami and be enveloped by the hug. Rebecca
was aware that it was the first hug she'd received in over a year.
Her skin swallowed the human touch eagerly, while she wept at
the realization of her isolation.

Rebecca spoke into Tami's shoulder, more for herself than to be heard. "I miss him every day, and even more when I'm sitting right next to him."

Tami gently released her tight grip around Rebecca but kept one arm linked over her shoulder as she drew back. She wished she could end the visit here, but the cloud of the nighttime issue kept flashing in Tami's mind.

"Can I tell you about your father's last two nights here?"

Rebecca knew something out of character must have happened, and part of her wanted to answer no. She didn't know if she could handle any more changes from the disease. Instead she nodded in agreement and braced herself.

"Your father has been wandering the halls at night and kissing the photographs of the other residents." Tami floated the statement delicately into the air and waited for any emotional fireworks.

Watching Rebecca's face closely, Tami was surprised to see a mix of relief and illumination flood her features. Rebecca's palm slapped her forehead with insight.

It was Tami's turn to be confused; this was not the reaction she had expected.

"I can't believe I forgot it. This is definitely fixable." Rebecca grinned, relief cascading through her being that her father hadn't transformed into a predator as everyone else had assumed. Rebecca turned and half ran towards the exit, oblivious to Tami and her gaping open mouth.

"Rebecca?" Tami called out trying to comprehend.

Rebecca turned briefly, still smiling, "I'll be back, ten minutes tops, you'll see."

Tami was frozen, unsure what was happening. She glanced at her watch, as she headed back in to see George, deciding to give Rebecca 15 minutes.

She took a seat on the bed, next to George, who sat staring blankly out the window. "So, you like to dance?" Tami thought she saw the faintest glimmer of a thought waltzing its way across George's brow. She followed his gaze out the window and added, "What is it that your daughter is getting that will solve this problem?"

✳✳✳

True to her word, Rebecca was back to George's room in ten minutes. She was out of breath and eager, carrying a frame in her hand. She immediately knelt in front of her father and held the framed 5 x 7 up for George to see. Tami eagerly leaned over to see what the mystery was.

There in the simple wooden frame was a black and white portrait of a boy. He was blond, with a buzzed haircut, and light-colored eyes. He wore a crisp white shirt and dark bow-tie. A missing front tooth gave his bold smile a bit of mischief.

George's face registered the photo, and the corners of his mouth turned upwards. He lifted his arm, feebly, and his bony finger pointed and reached until he made contact with the picture. He tapped the boy's face repeatedly.

"Who is that, Dad?"

Their attention turned to George whose lips moved into a pucker. Instinctively, Rebecca brought the photo up to George's mouth. He took hold of the frame, closed his eyes, and kissed the boy.

"Geoffrey." He said, with his eyes still locked on the image.

Rebecca patted her father's knee, her voice tender, "That's right. I'm so sorry that I forgot to pack the photo." Rebecca turned towards Tami, who was just starting to put the pieces together.

"That's a photo of my brother, Geoffrey. When he was eight, he and friends where swimming in a large creek at my grandparent's farm. It had rained the day before, and the creek was high and tortuous, and the boys wanted to float the creek. Geoff's foot got wedged in some branches," Rebecca looked back to her father as she finished, he seemed to be hanging on her words, "another boy, Frankie, tried to free him, but…." Rebecca couldn't continue.

Tami let the sorrow suspend in stillness, not wanting to disrupt the moment, while father and daughter connected in an unseen way.

The spell broke, and Rebecca turned again back to Tami, "Every night, Dad would talk to Geoffrey and give his photo a kiss before he went to sleep. As his dementia has worsened, the conversations have stopped, but the ritual remains."

Rebecca stood and took the frame from George, speaking to him as she placed it by his bed, "Dad, I'm putting Geoffrey right here." George's eyes followed, but he didn't speak.

Tami took this as her cue to exit. She felt light and full of air as she stood, excited to go share the narrative with Fran. "I will let the staff know that the wandering issue should be taken care of now."

Rebecca looked over to Tami, the skepticism and distrust had been washed completely away. The weariness still sat on her shoulders, but Tami heard the affection as Rebecca whispered, "Thank you."

4. VISITOR

Kathy

Delores was sitting in her easy chair, attempting to read Guidepost. In actuality, she was on the brink of falling asleep, when the wooden clock on the mantle chimed melodiously, announcing the seven o'clock hour. She blinked several times and rose from the chair, feeling weary. She was just 60, though her muscles and joints ached like an old woman.

"Blake, sweetie," she called out, guessing her four-year-old grandson was in his room playing dinosaurs. "Honey, it's seven o'clock, time to call your mom."

Blake's head peeked out of his room, looking down the hallway at his Grandma. "Ok, Mimi! I want to show her my t-rex, too."

Delores made sure to grab her cell phone off the coffee table as she headed into Blake's bedroom. The floor of the room was littered with plastic dinosaurs, set up in a battle of two opposing groups. The dinosaurs appeared to be organized based on color. Blake continued to fine tune the set-up, as Delores crossed to Blake's single bed and sat down. It often took her a moment to find the Face Time app and dial her son, Steve.

As soon as the familiar jingle of the phone connecting sounded, Blake leapt over the toys and landed on his bed with a jolt. He had his t-rex in hand and waited eagerly for his father's face.

Steve's face appeared on the phone and Blake immediately began to speak, "Hi Dad! Look, my t-rex is getting ready to win a battle against the greens." At this, Blake made a growling sound for the dinosaur.

"That's great buddy," Steve replied, "you ready to say goodnight to mom?" Blake nodded, as his dad brought the phone and camera in front of his mother's face. Kathy lay in a hospital bed, her eyes open and the left side of her face drooping. She was gaunt, weighing just 80 pounds, and had delicate features. Distracted by her contorted arms and legs, bent and rigid from multiple strokes, most who saw her ignored her soft brown eyes and hair.

Blake, however, didn't think it was strange at all. He had only ever known his mom to be like this. Kathy was diagnosed with lung cancer just months after Blake was born. She and Steve had spent the first few weeks after the diagnosis in shock, still adjusting to being first time parents. They began treatment immediately, determined to beat the cancer. Delores had moved to Kansas City immediately, to help with Blake, as the therapy was aggressive and time consuming.

After eight months of chemotherapy, Kathy had her first stroke. She had awoken one morning, unable to move the right side of her body. They had to put the chemotherapy on hold, and Kathy entered rehab to try and regain her function and relearn to walk. Delores took Blake to the rehab center often. Blake was just learning to take his first steps, and they tried to enjoy the humor of both infant and mother learning to walk.

Someone had snapped a photo one day of Kathy standing behind her walker smiling, and Blake next to her, holding on to the metal walker leg with his chubby little hands, grinning with pride. Steve had the photo framed. He had thought the photo would be something to look back on one day with a satisfied sense of victory, once they'd won their cancer battle. He never dreamed that the photo would immortalize the best Kathy ever got.

A few weeks after that photo was taken, she had another stroke. The doctors explained that it was the cancer causing these strokes. The family was determined to get her strong enough to take more chemotherapy, so the rehab was extended.

Kathy couldn't walk after the second stroke but could still communicate. It took an entire year until she was well enough to start the aggressive chemo again.

Although the strokes had left Kathy debilitated, when Blake turned three, it looked as if the cancer was in remission. Kathy used a motorized wheel chair in their home, and Blake's favorite activity was getting rides around the house. Delores continued to live with the family, helping with Kathy and Blake, which allowed Steve to return to his work as a financial advisor.

This reprieve was short lived, and at a three month follow up scan with their oncologist, they found that the tumor was back, and back with a vengeance.

If Delores, Steve, or Kathy, had any doubts about starting chemotherapy again, they didn't communicate it. With almost audible creaking, the well-oiled treatment engine that they had perfected, started up again.

Shortly after treatment started, Kathy had her third stroke. This one destroyed her ability to talk and left her unable to use her upper arms. Even though their hopes and wishes for a full recovery seemed to ooze out of their pores, Kathy began to regress both physically and emotionally. Ultimately, hospice was called in, and as her symptoms worsened, they moved her into the Hospice House.

"Hi, Mom!" Blake spoke to Kathy as he would to anyone on the phone. Kathy's eyelids fluttered, but she could give no other response. Blake continued, "Mom, see my t-rex? He is going to chomp up the other dinosaurs. He is so strong." Blake did his roaring imitation again, and Delores could be heard trying to hush him in the background and redirect him to the task at hand. "Well, goodnight Mom, love you. I hope you feel better tomorrow."

A tinge of guilt flooded Steve. He had not been honest with Blake about Kathy's condition. How, though, could he explain to his four-year-old that his mother was dying? He shoved the uncomfortable thought down and brought the phone back to his face. "Goodnight Buddy, glad you called. I'm going to talk to Grandma a minute, okay?"

Blake easily went back to his dinosaur battle, and Delores deliberately stepped out of Blake's room for privacy.

"Mom," Steve continued with concern sneaking into his words, "the nurses mentioned something about seeing some color changes on Kathy's feet tonight."

"Oh? What do you mean?"

"It's a funny word they used, something with an M. But they pointed it out; her toes are purple."

"That just sounds like being cold to me," Delores brushed off the concern.

"Maybe, but they seemed to think it meant something." Steve hesitated, and then continued, "I was wondering if you could bring Blake up tomorrow, just in case."

Delores didn't like changing the routine, but reluctantly agreed. She also didn't want to linger on the phone, sensing Steve's fragility tonight. "Try to get some sleep, Steve. I'd better go get Blake to bed."

"Thanks Mom" Steve thought about saying more, expressing more of his immense gratitude for the life his Mother had given up helping her only son and grandson. Perhaps sensing this in his pause, Delores abruptly said goodnight and hung up.

✲✲✲

Kathy had been living at the Hospice House for 3 weeks, and Blake was very familiar with the place. When Delores pulled into a spot in the circle drive near the portico overhang, Blake immediately undid his car seat straps and opened the back door of Delores's Cadillac.

"Blake, you wait for me, and watch for cars!" Delores admonished. Blake paused, shifting his 3 dinosaurs in his arms trying to negotiate shutting the car door.

"Okay," he said with annoyance.   Normally at this time, Blake would have been in preschool, and he was excited with the change of schedule.

Delores searched for other cars as she came around the front to Blake's side. Seeing nothing, she gave a nod of permission to Blake. With this, Blake sprinted across the drive, through the large double oak doors, and out of Delores's sight.

By the time Delores made it down the long hallway to room 16, Blake had already set up his three plastic companions on the seat of the chair next to Kathy's bed, and was kneeling on the floor absorbed in play.

Delores went immediately to Kathy, taking her hand and spoke cheerfully, "Good morning, dear! You look like you've had a bath this morning." Delores tucked a few strands of Kathy's thinned dark hair behind her ear. Kathy, meanwhile, didn't move. Her eyes were open, and she seemed to gaze at a spot in the ceiling. Delores continued to speak to her daughter-in-law, filling the quietness with mundane chatter.

There was a slight knock on the door to the room, and Angela, one of the nurses, came in. Angela smiled warmly, "I thought I saw a blur running down the hall, and sure enough, Blake is here."

Blake paused momentarily and glanced up with a mischievous grin. Delores was assertive as she addressed Angela, "Has Kathy had breakfast yet this morning? I don't see the tray in here or any signs she's had anything."

Angela reminded herself that Delores meant well, as she replied, "Well, actually Steve and I both discussed it before he left for work and didn't think it was a good idea this morning."

"Not a good idea? What does that mean? I'm sure she's half-starved this morning, and she cannot afford to lose any more weight."

"Actually, it's the swallowing that's the problem. Last night she choked and coughed with dinner. It was hard for Steve to see her in distress, so he brought up that we…"

Delores interrupted, "I doubt she was actually choking. People usually just don't know the proper way to help feed Kathy.

I've been doing it for months now. If you'll have someone bring in some oatmeal and orange juice, I'd appreciate it."

Angela felt it was better not to argue and knew this was a battle she would not win. Politely she conceded, "I'd be happy to do that. Though, Delores, you may find things significantly different today. Kathy hasn't had any urine out since last night, and as you can tell, she's not very responsive today." Delores had already turned back to Kathy as Angela spoke, so Angela did not see Delores squeeze her eyes shut with this information, as if attempting to will away the negative news.

As Angela slipped out, Delores began to speak again to Kathy in a mothering tone. "No food! I bet you are hungry! How can we keep you strong if you don't eat?"

In no time, Angela was back with a tray carrying the things Delores had requested. She helped Delores get Kathy heaved up in bed and raised to a sitting position. Kathy's muscle tone precluded her from sitting, so pillows were used to keep her from toppling to the side. Her neck quickly drifted towards her right shoulder and more pillows were placed.

Blake rose from his playing, "Mimi, can I go play in the kid's area. I don't like watching mommy eat." Delores frowned at this admission but agreed he could have some time in the play area Hospice had set up for kids, just a few rooms down from this one.

Angela stepped back towards the door but didn't leave. She wanted to see how the feeding process would go.

Delores was confidant, as she used her thumb and first finger to pinch and pick up a small amount of thick oatmeal. Positioning her left hand behind Kathy's neck, she moved the food into the pocket of Kathy's right cheek. The movement reminded Angela of hand feeding an infant.

"Now come on, Kathy, you need to swallow, Honey. You must be hungry, and this is yummy!"

Angela grimaced at the process and waited to see what would happen. Kathy had, from start to finish of this ordeal, made no movement on her own. Delores was stroking Kathy's cheek and chin to attempt to cue her to swallow. Enough of the morsel of food must have made its way into Kathy's throat, as a guttural choking sound ensued. The cough was weak but rhythmic, just like any spasmodic cough that happens when something goes into the windpipe rather than getting swallowed.

Delores changed her cajoling chatter to Kathy about eating, to a pep talk about coughing, "Come on, Kathy! Cough it up! That's right, get it out of there." As she encouraged Kathy, with her left hand she forcefully patted Kathy's back. Eerily, Angela was once again reminded of how similar these actions were to feeding an infant.

The sputtering cough slowed and stopped, and both Angela and Delores visibly relaxed. Besides the coughing, Kathy remained lifeless throughout the ordeal. "I think we'll try later, maybe she's just not quite awake enough." Delores stated, not wanting to admit defeat.

Angela kindly came to the bedside and silently helped Delores position Kathy back to a reclining position. She put a hand on Delores's shoulder and said, "I am glad you brought Blake today." The implication of Angela's tone settled on Delores momentarily, and then she shrugged Angela's hand off, bristling.

"Kathy is clearly exhausted today. I think we will leave in a bit to allow her to rest and get her strength up."

Angela nodded her acknowledgment of the statement without agreeing with Delores. "One last thing," Angela timidly mentioned, "our Chaplain, Lou, is here this morning. Would you like him to stop in to visit?"

Delores's head snapped around towards Angela sharply, "Thank you, but no. I can't think of any way a Chaplain could be helpful at this point." Her tone was dismissive and final.

Angela nodded and quietly left. Delores said under her breath, "If God was going to be of any help, he'd have shown up way back at the beginning of this mess."

✶✶✶

The sun had set, and Delores was washing dishes from her and Blake's dinner. The change in schedule for the day had been a disaster for Blake. Delores tried to think how many times she had sent Blake to time-out. Was it five or six, she pondered, rehearsing the reprimanding conversation she would have with her son, Steve, that night. "I need to remind Steve not to lose hope and not to panic with every little change." Delores spoke out loud to herself, letting the water run over the ceramic plate she held.

Her mind began to wander. She thought back to nearly five years ago, when Kathy and Steve had announced their pregnancy. That year had been such a dark year; her divorce had been finalized with Steve's dad, James. Her own mother had died suddenly after a long hospital stay with pneumonia. She had spent weeks wondering what the point of her own life was and if she would ever find happiness again. Then she got the phone call from Steve and Kathy that they were expecting. She recalled the elation she felt, and the news filled a deep void within her. This baby will be my purpose, she had thought.

That impulsive wish became much more real when Kathy

was diagnosed with lung cancer. Delores couldn't admit it to anyone, but she felt renewed by being able to swoop in and take care of Steve, Kathy, and Blake.

"Mimi!" Blake's little voice snapped Delores back to the present. She quickly turned off the water that had been running for minutes on end and set the plate in the drying rack.

"Blake, dear, don't yell, I'm right here."

"But Mimi, the lotion spilled on the carpet."

"Blake Steven!" Delores didn't hide her irritation, "Where and why did the lotion spill?" She quickly dried her hands on a tea towel and strode towards Blake, who had already turned and was pointing to the hall bathroom.

"I was just trying to help my army man get better, like mom. I was putting on the lotion medicine and it all came out in a blob." Blake said sheepishly.

Delores passed him with a 'humph' and peered into the bathroom with her arms on her hips. Her shoulders sagged as she took in a golf ball sized globule of pink lotion matted into the fringed carpet. She fought her impulse to scold Blake, as she noted the toy army man lying on a wash cloth and several other action figures positioned around him as if in a hospital.

"Blake, just…" Delores paused trying to decide if she should have him clean it up. "…just, go play in your room please, I'll get this." She decided it would be easier to do it herself.

Delores spent more time than she wanted scrubbing the oily lotion out of the carpet. When she was finally satisfied, she eased herself up from the floor, feeling each and every muscle protest the change in position.

She hobbled into the den, her right knee still locked up from being on the floor. She collapsed into her recliner, just as the clock chimed the seven o'clock hour. Delores groaned inwardly, not wanting to rise from her chair.

"Blake!" Delores called, deciding he could come to her to-night, "Honey, it's time to call your mom." Delores noticed her phone was on the end table next to her, and mumbled, "Thank you."

There was no response from Blake, so she called out again, a little louder this time. She paused to listen carefully, thinking perhaps he would shout something in response, but only the heavy ticking of the clock on the mantle was heard.

Getting frustrated, she called a third time, "Blake Steven! I need you in the den now!" She could feel the exasperation turning to anger as Blake remained missing. "That boy!" Delores groaned, pushing her over-tired body up from the recliner. She paused once she was standing to massage her right leg, which was still stiff, calling out a final warning, "Blake, this is your last chance. If I have to come to your room, you're going to be in big trouble!"

Her anger was tinged with slight concern now. Blake was ornery, but not usually outright disobedient.

She headed down the hallway towards the closed door of Blake's room, a question to her tone now, "Blake? Honey, what are you doing?"

Just as she reached for the door knob to his bedroom, the door was drawn open suddenly, Blake and Delores both startled by each other's presence.

"Mimi!" Blake beamed, "What are you doing?"

Delores's anger returned now that she saw Blake was not only okay, but almost jovial. "Didn't you hear me calling you? What have you been doing? It's well past time now to call your Mother!"

"It's okay, Mimi," Blake seemed to be dismissive as he turned back towards his action figures on the floor.

"Excuse me, young man, it is not okay! Your mother and father will be expecting a goodnight call."

Blake turned back towards his grandmother and tilted his head to the side, "No! I mean I don't need to call her tonight, because she came to see me here," Blake pointed towards his bed and continued matter-of-factly, "she even told me goodnight and that she loved me." Blake's face was full of adoration and happiness.

Delores felt the hairs on her neck stand and her heart skipped a beat. A hand reflexively covered her open mouth. Before she could think to call Steve, the cellphone in her other hand began to vibrate.

Still watching Blake in a trance like state, she answered her phone, barely able to squeak out a, "Hello."

"Mom," Steve's anguished voice called out on the line, "She's gone." Unable to hold back his grief, she could hear him crying through the phone.

"I know." The softness in her tone surprised Steve, who had expected disbelief and shock. At least that was the emotion he was dealing with as he felt a tight squeezing in his chest that he assumed was grief.

"But how…"

Steve's confusion was cut off by a child's voice. Blake had intuitively known his grandmother was talking to his dad and had taken the phone out of her hands. Delores, still unable to process all that had taken place in the last ten minutes, gave up the phone willingly.

"Dad!" Blake said with innocent excitement, "Mom came to see me!" Blake's own enthusiasm settled into a more serious note, as he recounted, "She told me she had to tell me goodbye, but that things would be okay."

Large uncontrolled sobs overtook Steve's body, unable to pull it together to speak to his son. He was awash with both the realization of his loss, and the simultaneous sweetness of what his son had experienced. He looked over at the still shell of a body that was his wife and could hear the words Kathy spoke to Blake sear themselves into his own consciousness; it would have to be okay.

5. TRAPPED

Scott

DING! DING! DING! The wonky doorbell sounded. "You have got to be kidding me," Shelby mumbled, irritated and rolling her eyes. She grunted, shoving herself up from the ratty gold and brown couch and looked over at her husband. "This is your fault, you know!" Her eyes narrowing as she trudged to the door.

Her husband, Scott made a guttural sound from his wheelchair positioned next to the couch. His neck and head remained in a rigid posture resting against the high winged support extending off the top of the wheelchair. He could hear voices from the front door 15 feet away, but their large 60-inch flat screen TV obscured his view. On the TV, a fight broke out between the guests of the Jerry Springer show, the noise drowning out what Shelby and whoever was at the door were saying.

Scott hated Jerry Springer. He eyed the remote on the couch out of the corner of his eye. He knew he could not move his arm to reach it, but his brain still went through the effort of trying. His index finger moved upwards and then back down. That's all I'm going to get, he thought to himself.

"Scott!" Shelby announced cheerfully, as his eyes moved from watching his one mobile finger dance to the two new women walking towards him with Shelby. "Look who is here! It's the new hospice people, come to save the day!"

The taller of the two came forward, "Hi, Scott. My name is Tami and I'm a nurse with Kansas City Hospice." Scott found Tami's brown eyes gentle, and inwardly he relaxed. He placed her around his age, early 50s. Tami continued, "...and this is Ruth, who is one of our social workers." Ruth, younger at 30, smiled sincerely and gave a short wave in greeting.

Shelby motioned for the hospice workers to sit on the couch, and then went directly behind Scott and protectively placed her hands on his shoulders. "We weren't really sure if we needed more help," adding, "isn't that right, honey?" Her look was a bit dubious as she explained, "I've been Scott's only caregiver and I'm with him twenty-four hours a day. He really does not like new people." At this, Shelby began running her hands back and forth across Scott's back. "We have our routine down and it works so well."

Tami cleared her throat sensing a need to earn Shelby's approval. "Yes, indeed, you are the one who knows and cares for Scott best." At this Tami pointedly looked to Scott to shift the conversation. "Scott, as you know, when you were in the hospital last week with pneumonia things were pretty serious." Tami waited to see if Scott would respond. There was a slight movement of Scott's head as he tried to nod.

Shelby interjected, "Oh, I bet you didn't know, but Scott can't talk. He blinks once for yes and twice for no. I also have learned to perceive what he wants; I've been with him so long, you know."

"Thank you," Tami half smiled at Shelby, and then turned her attention back to Scott. "I understand that you were diagnosed with ALS three years ago, but that things really started to accelerate in the last three months, is that correct?"

Scott blinked once as Shelby jumped in, "It's been so fast! Three months ago he was still talking and now I'm feeding him through a tube in his stomach." At this statement, Shelby wrinkled her nose a bit.

Scott felt a wave of shame flood over him. The doctors had warned him that Lou Gehrig's disease, the lay term for ALS, would be difficult. The slow loss of strength was agonizing. First, it was just weakness, and then he lost his ability to walk, stand, and use his arms. The swallowing and talking had been challenging and once those were gone, he lost his desire to keep living. When the doctors in the hospital explained that he was losing the ability to breathe on his own, which had complicated his pneumonia, they offered him two choices. He could have a surgical hole placed in his neck and be hooked up to a respirator that would breathe for him, or he could focus on making the end comfortable by bringing hospice on board. The decision for him was simple.

Scott tried to refocus. He had not been paying attention, and Tami was ending her sentence, "…specializing in symptom management and supportive care." Scott blinked once and Tami continued, "I will come visit for an assessment twice a week initially, and Ruth will come once a week. Hospice will now cover all of your medications and any equipment you need."

Shelby let out an audible sigh. "I am happy to hear that.

Things have been really tight financially!"

Tami moved the conversation along, explaining that a hospice aide would also be available to help with personal care needs. Shelby leaned forward to look at Scott, "Aren't you lucky Scott! Someone else besides me to get you all cleaned up. I hope they will do as good as me!" A flash of hesitancy appeared in Scott's facial expression.

Tami interpreted this as best she could and reached for Scott's arm in a protective gesture. "Scott, I know it must be incredibly difficult to lose your independence and control over the most basic things. I want you to know that we want to help. We know you did not choose this. It would be a privilege for us to care for you."

Scott felt a tear escape from his eye and had no ability to wipe it off. Tami's words washed over him in a soothing way. He wanted to believe that he was not at fault for he and Shelby's current situation but could not. Shelby reminded him often that he was ruining her life. It was true, he was.

Shelby and Scott had met at AJ's Roofing Company 11 years ago. She worked in the front office answering phones when Scott was hired for the roofing crew. They were both raw from recent breakups and Shelby's straight-shooting bluntness was in perfect contrast to his mild mannered shy self. Scott was 40 when they met, Shelby just 28. Her spunkiness made him feel much younger and they were married within six months, and six months after that he had convinced her that they should start their own roofing company.

For seven years, he had put in 60-hour workweeks, trying to build up his business and pay off his start-up costs. It was during that seventh year when things looked like they would finally be profitable that his right hand started to stiffen up, and he had trouble deploying the nail gun. The diagnosis was terrible: amy-otrophic lateral sclerosis. Within the year he was unable to work, and with medical bills piling up, he had to liquidate the company. Things had gone downhill from there.

The hospice team stayed another 30 minutes going through his medications and routines. Shelby signed the paper work authorizing hospice to treat him. Though the long meeting wore Scott out, he felt less anxious than he had for weeks.

Scott dozed on and off the rest of the afternoon. He had only been home from the hospital two days, but things were significantly worse. He spent his days propped in his custom motorized wheelchair, and before his last hospitalization, he had enough strength in his finger and hand to move the joystick control and propel himself around their small home. Now, despite his greatest effort and concentration all he could get was a flick, causing the wheelchair to jerk forward or sideways. It was reminiscent of learning to drive a clutch, sputtering and halting but going nowhere. This annoyed Shelby to no end. "Would you just get over here already?" She would yell whenever she had some task Scott needed help with.

Shelby had been on her phone more than usual, distracted and amused by whomever she was texting. Scott had a cramp in his right thigh from being in the same position for hours and was trying to get her attention any way he could. His soft grunts were to no avail, so he decided to use the wheelchair's short bursts.

This tactic worked in getting Shelby's attention but in the wrong way. "What!?!" Shelby barked, "Can I not have 5 minutes of peace for myself? I cannot even have a conversation with anyone without you interrupting!" Scott tried to rock his trunk and opened his eyes as wide as possible to indicate what he needed. Shelby, though, never took her face from the phone, her fingers moving across the keys as she rose from the couch.

"Look," she said, finally glancing up and at him, "I need a break. I am about to lose my mind sitting around here all day. I am going to give you a can of Ensure and some pain meds, and then I'm going to go meet a friend for a drink." She quickly looked away, avoiding the pleading look in Scott's eyes.

She was going to leave him alone? Fear welled up like a tidal wave and Scott's vocalizations became more rapid. On her way to the kitchen to get his nutrition she called back "Come on, don't give me that. You don't do anything anyways - but just sit there."

After feeding Scott the liquid nutrition through the tube in his stomach Shelby went to get ready. She changed clothes and put on make-up, pulling her dirty blond hair back into a ponytail. Despite the growing fear, Scott felt a pang of longing when she entered the living room. She really was beautiful and the sparkle in her eyes and her flushed skin reminded him of their heady first six months together. As if Shelby could sense Scott's longing and in a final attempt to assuage any tinge of guilt, Shelby turned the TV on to the History Channel and grinned at Scott. "See, you'll get to watch your favorite channel while I'm gone. You are going to have a blast!"

She left the main lights on as she walked out the front door. The 'thunk' the door made when it closed seemed to penetrate into Scott's limbs. He could feel his heart pounding rapidly in his chest as 'what ifs' played across his mind. Slowly he sensed a drowsiness begin to settle inwardly. He wondered how much morphine she had given him with his meal, while simultaneously the apathy of the opioid took over and he did not really care. Soon he was in a medicated sleep dreaming of the time before ALS.

✶✶✶

In the few moments before full consciousness, Scott was aware that someone had propped him up in his bed. He searched his memory for when Shelby had come home or when she moved him into their room, but only blankness greeted him. He opened his eyes and could see Shelby's form to his right, the smell of cigarette smoke lingered on her as she snored loudly. He let his gaze drift forward to the dresser and mirror at the foot of the bed. Gone was the tanned, muscular man he had been. A stranger with hollow cheeks, sagging pale skin and sad eyes looked at him. He squeezed his eyes tightly shut, willing away the vision of himself.

Shelby's cell phone vibrated on the nightstand next to her. She let out an irritated sigh as she stirred and blindly reached for her phone to answer a call. Shelby greeted the unknown caller with an annoyed, "What?" and then, "Oh, hospice, yes, hi. He's fine," she said, her tone immediately sweet and accommodating. She moved her head to glance at Scott, a fake smile plastered on her face. "This morning?" she asked, "Sure that would be fine." Shelby did her best to disguise a loud yawn as she pulled herself up to a sitting position. "I was just getting ready to bathe him, but you want me to hold off until you arrive?" She smiled at the answer on the line, then closed the conversation and hung up.

Ignoring Scott, Shelby left the room to shower. Scott wrestled with conflicting thoughts knowing that hospice was on its way. Part of him was looking forward to a bed bath. Shelby certainly had not bathed him for days, and he could smell his own malodorous scent. At the same time, he was apprehensive, he had always been modest and was not looking forward to the lack of privacy involved with personal hygiene help.

Tami and the new hospice aide, Beth, stayed for over an hour. Scott had not felt that fresh and clean in over a month. They bathed him, washed his hair, and shaved his face. They even trimmed his nails. Tami commented on some deep purple areas on Scott's backside, implying that he had been sitting in the same position for too long. Tami brought Shelby into the bedroom to point out the spots, as well as some areas on his upper arm. Tami kindly used it as an education moment, talking to Shelby about proper ways to lift Scott and the importance of shifting his weight in the chair every few hours.

Scott was relieved the nurse was addressing this, but when he looked over at Shelby for her response, he grew tense. Shelby acted befuddled and gracious, "I certainly appreciate the education, Tami. I am not sure how those spots got there!" Shelby's gaze met Scott's and he saw anger in her eyes.

Sure enough, after the hospice team left, Shelby let loose. Her tone dripped with nasty sarcasm, "Well, Scott, I see you're doing it again, making sure I am well loved and respected."

Hospice had left Scott seated in his wheelchair out in the living room. He watched as Shelby paced in front of him, her face in a snarl. "Now, I'm the idiot. Apparently, I cannot take care of you correctly." She continued to circle and attack him with her words. His inability to argue back deflated the situation more quickly than long arguments they had had in the past. As was typical, Shelby concluded her rant escaping to the kitchen. He could hear her set a glass angrily on the counter and the vodka sloshing into it. He had seen her do this a hundred times and pictured her head back as she inhaled the shot. He knew to scale her wrath by how many drinks she put back. One, clank and slosh, two, clank and slosh, three, clank; She was livid.

Just then, there was a knock on the door. "Can you get that,

Scott?" Shelby laughed sardonically. She came through the kitchen to the doorway, now in the line of sight of Scott. "Oh, no? You don't want to help today? Let me then." She flung open the door and saw the mail carrier retreating and a large box on the stoop with the rest of their mail lying on top.

She took the three pieces of mail in one hand and pulled the package into the entry with the other hand. "It's our lucky day, Scott, diapers!" She kicked the lightweight box past the TV and up to the front of Scott's wheelchair, knocking the box into his feet purposefully. "Let's see what else we have," Shelby waved the envelopes in front of Scott's face. The alcohol was beginning to take effect and Shelby's movements became more exaggerated.

She opened the thickest envelope. Scott had seen the logo of the hospital when she waved it before his eyes. As he feared, it was another bill, this one from a hospitalization over a month ago.

Shelby's eyes grew large and then narrowed as she scanned the invoice. "Twelve-thousand dollars, Scott! Add that to the twenty-thousand we still owe, and we've got ourselves a nightmare."

The room was silent; Shelby stood staring at the bill. Her hand began to grip the paper more tightly causing the letter to begin to wrinkle. The reminder of their desperate financial strain was the oxygen to the already brewing ember of anger from the humiliation earlier in the day.

Very dramatically, Shelby let the paper drop to the floor, and she looked directly into Scott's eyes. The loathing he saw there sent a shiver up his spine. "You don't even care, do you? I do all the work, for what?" There was a long pause.

When she broke the silence, her voice was eerily quiet, yet determined as she proclaimed, "I did not ask for this." She gestured at him, and to their small house, and finally at the box of Depends between them. "You have managed to ruin my life." Bitterness dripped from each word.

Her verbal assaults were a common occurrence, but this felt different to Scott. She continued, "I cannot do this any longer." She paused, her upper lip raised in disgust, "I will NOT do this any longer."

She methodically turned, walked around the back of the couch and into their bedroom at the rear of the house. Scott's brows knit together in confusion, and as he attempted to vocalize and turn his wheelchair towards their bedroom, his breathing quickened.

Suddenly the shattering sound of a gunshot shook the entire house. For a moment, Scott's heart seemed to stop beating. The home immediately grew deathly quiet. A wave of adrenaline and terror interrupted the shock, as Scott's eyes grew to the size of saucers and he let out a loud cry. In his mind, he screamed, "Shelby, Shelby! Are you okay?" His one working finger pulsated as he attempted to knock the joystick anyway that he could.

He was even weaker today and could not even push with enough force to get a jerk. He was crying now, picturing the scene in his mind. He imagined Shelby across their bed in a pool of blood. His guttural sounds took the shape of actual words, as he cried, "No!" repeatedly.

Lost in an agonizing prison of helplessness, Scott was not conscious of time's passage until headlights from a passing car outside, blinded him. It was completely dark in the home. Simultaneously, he became aware of several things: He hurt. It was hard to breathe. He was alone. He was terrified.

Never had he longed for his own death more than now. He could not sleep, though he was exhausted. His physical discomfort was only half of the problem, for just as he would begin to drift off, he would startle, thinking he heard a gunshot and reliving the reality of his situation.

✳✳✳

Eventually morning came and the house lightened, though there was no joy in the dawn of this new day. He had no more tears, though his mouth still opened with silent cries every few minutes.

In the midst of his ongoing agony, there was a sound at the front door. In that instant, Scott remembered about hospice, and prayed that their door would be unlocked. Feeling like a shipwrecked sailor who just spotted a life preserver, for the first time in hours there was a glimmer of hope.

He watched the doorknob turn and the door open without hesitation. Scott choked and forced himself to blink several times when his brain registered Shelby standing in the entryway. She closed the door behind her, nonchalantly, and took a step into the living room. Her smile was amused, "I just got a call from hospice, and they will be here to see you in a few minutes. I thought I had better be 'home' when they came."

Fresh tears streamed down Scott's face. "What's wrong, Scott? It looks like you've seen a ghost!" Shelby smirked and made her way into the kitchen. Scott's renewed shock, horror, and anger wrapped around his chest like a clamp. He began to cough and sputter, his breathing labored. Before Shelby had a chance to ridicule him more, the doorbell rang.

Shelby called out, "Come in." Tami entered and immediately noticed Scott's distress, rushing to his side and moving the box of

Depends out of the way.

"Shelby, when was Scott's last dose of morphine and how long has he been breathing like this?" she called with urgency in her voice.

Shelby poked her head around the corner feigning surprise, "Wow! Must have just started, he's been absolutely fine since you all left yesterday." Shelby caught Scott's panicked gaze and winked, disappearing into the kitchen again.

Tami continued to talk to Scott, "Scott, we are going to help this. I am sure it is frightening not being able to catch your breath! I am so glad I decided to check on you today, my intuition said you needed a visit!" Tami quickly took control of the situation getting a dose of morphine through his feeding tube and checking his vitals.

Tami had seen the look of terror in Scott's eyes when she arrived and even after the medication began to slow down his breathing the look was still present. As Tami examined Scott and assessed him, she commented, "You almost seem to be in the same spot we left you in yesterday morning. Also, I hate saying this, but it sure looks like you've been through hell!" Scott caught Tami's eye and with as much force as possible did an exaggerated blink. Tami paused and looked deep into Scott's eyes. He felt she was looking into him and seeing a glimpse of what terrified him. His brain screamed, "Help me!"

He saw a wave of understanding pass over her face and she took hold of his upper arm. "Scott, I think it's time we made arrangements for you to come to the Hospice House. The way you've been breathing, the way you look today, I think things are changing quickly and I think you need the 24-hour intensive care the Hospice House offers."

Tears once again fell from Scott's eyes, this time in gratitude.

Things moved quickly from there on; an ambulance called, papers signed. Shelby feigned concern, but a definite note of joy surrounded her words. She told hospice that she had some important things to take care of, but that she would visit Scott later in the evening.

Once admitted to room 14, he felt peace settle upon him. The nurse informed him that Shelby had called and would not be able to visit that night. He guessed he would not see her again. As he lay there, he tried to convince himself that the last 24 hours was a nightmare, simultaneously trying to heal the wound Shelby had caused by her psychological trick. He guessed the current time was ten in the morning and his body begged for slumber. He closed his eyes, giving in to the exhaustion, and thought he heard the distant sound of a violin wafting through his walls as he drifted off to sleep. His last thoughts were yearning for the freedom he hoped death would bring.

6. CHOICES

Lilian

Lilian sat at her well-worn kitchen table tapping the end of her ballpoint pen mindlessly. She was surrounded by bills and correspondence that had been placed in her to-do pile. Her intentions were good; she had gathered her checkbook and envelopes, determined to take care of this today. But just like the previous several mornings, the knot in the pit of her stomach was distracting. She was sure it was stress. She felt overwhelmed knowing the bills in her stack demanded more than the money in her and Nick's checking account. She had looked at their balance every day, as if by merely wishing they had more money it would suddenly appear.

The sound of the garage door hummed the tune of opening, bringing Lilian a much needed interruption from her spiraling thoughts. She turned expectantly towards the garage entry door, as the blur of her youngest daughter, Charlotte, bombarded into the house.

"Char?" Lillian questioned, "What are you doing home?"

Already past the kitchen, a muffled voice yelled back, "My Calc book." Seconds later Charlotte was back in the kitchen, textbook in hand. "I forgot my book and homework, and Mr. Gruber told me last week he'd start knocking my grade for late work." Charlotte stood with her hand on the door knob, straight blond hair parted on the side, with self-confidence oozing from her pores, as seniors often had.

"Sweetie, I could have run it up. How did you get permission to leave?"

Charlotte rolled her eyes, "Mom, seriously? It's fine. I like having the chance to get out. Plus, that stomach thing of yours, I didn't want to bother you."

Lilian looked perplexed, "What stomach thing?"

"I'm not stupid, sheesh, I can tell you've been hurting, and you seem sick and all." Charlotte's eyes glanced to the clock hanging above Lilian. "Sorry, got to go, see ya."

Without even a chance to respond, the door shut forcefully, and she heard the engine of the old Honda Civic start up.

Lillian put her hand across her stomach, speaking out loud to herself, "Have I really been acting sick?" The realization that the pain she'd been fighting for weeks now, was obvious to her daughter, scared her a little. She wondered if it was time to make a doctor's appointment. "But that would be one more bill to pay," she mumbled under her breath. She inhaled and drew her attention back to the papers in front of her.

On top was a bill from the K-State Campus Store with hundreds of dollars due. Lilian's other two children, Clarissa and Anson were both at K-State. She and Nick had argued for months before Anson started college about what parents should contribute. They settled on paying textbook fees only, which Lilian realized now, was even a stretch for them.

With one hand kneading the dull ache in her stomach and the other writing checks, Lilian resigned herself to a painful morning.

✶✶✶

Lillian stood at the stove top stirring the broccoli au gratin rice dish, the cardboard box next to the skillet betraying the sophistication of the dinner she prepared for she and Nick. She glanced in the oven at the two chicken breasts baking and looked at the clock. She expected to hear her husband any minute.

As she stirred the rice, a wave of guilt swept over her. What a poor wife I am, not even able to fix something more challenging than this, she thought. She used to put much more effort into evening meals. In fact, when all three children were still at home, the evening meal was the centerpiece of the day. Somehow, despite sports practices and other school activities, they almost always managed to sit and eat together. It was Lilian's unyielding determination for this priority which had made it happen.

The garage door opened, and moments later Nick came in. He was in business attire for his job as a court clerk and carried in his arms a few manila folders. He greeted Lilian warmly as he made his way past the kitchen to their bedroom where he would hang up his coat and tie.

She readied their plates and drinks and was sitting at the table when he entered the kitchen.

"Smells good," he said, taking his seat opposite his wife. He looked over at Lilian, concern clouding his expression. "Lil, you don't look so good."

Lilian's plastered smile that she had worked hard to present faded. "Sorry," she apologized, "just a rough day."

His eyes squinted and his head cocked, imploring more explanation.

She was feeling vulnerable and jumped right into the heart of most of her thoughts during the day. "It's just," she surveyed the kitchen as she spoke, "this, my life." She paused, "I'm 50 years old, and we are still struggling to pay our bills! I thought by now I would be able to finally relax."

"Lil," Nick started in protest, but Lilian gave him a look that said to back off.

"If I had just decided to go to medical school, think how different things would be for us!"

Nick sighed, "Not this again. Lilian that was over 20 years ago."

"I know, I know. But even this stomach pain, I was thinking how, if I was a doctor, I'd know exactly how to feel better, and I wouldn't have to pay someone else for that information!"

"You were pregnant! What option did you have?"

"No, Nick, that's not an excuse! Maybe I could have done both? Plenty of people have children during medical school."

Nick began to get agitated and his voice carried his frustration, "Are we seriously going to rehash this again? We have talked this in circles already. Think back. Don't you remember? That decision was extremely thought out!"

How could Lilian forget? They had been married 3 years and were struggling to connect emotionally. She had been pregnant twice and lost both babies in the first trimester. He was unfazed by the two losses and didn't understand why Lilian needed to grieve. Lilian, on the other hand, was devastated. In an effort to steel her hurting heart she had decided to pursue her dream of becoming a doctor and give up on being a parent.

The same week she received her acceptance letter to medical school, the pregnancy test she'd bought on a whim read "positive." While the acceptance letter had brought immediate pride and exultation to them both, the pregnancy test had enveloped her with fear. In the coming days as she adjusted to the idea of being pregnant and hesitantly let the seed of hope grow, she found that the fortified barrier she'd placed against the idea of motherhood begin to crumble. Her gut predicted that she wouldn't be able to do both. A decision needed to be made.

For several evenings in a row, Nick and she had walked around their neighborhood of tiny starter homes. Nick had listened to Lilian process the looming decision but didn't push her one way or the other. As they walked, Lilian's eyes seemed to zero in on tricycles, soccer balls, plastic toys, and other evidences of childhood littering the yards and driveways around her. The desire to be a mother pulsated inside, and she made her decision.

Lilian came back to reality and looked down at her dinner, not wanting to meet Nick's gaze. "Yes, I remember. All I'm saying is that maybe I could have done both."

Nick began to eat in silence. Lilian's pondering the past wasn't anything new. She brought up the abandoned medical school dream several times a year; enough so, that both Clarissa and Anson enrolled at K-state as pre-med majors.

Nick watched Lilian take a bite. She averted his scrutiny. He noticed that she winced as she swallowed a morsel of chicken. Suddenly the irritation Nick held dissipated.

"Are you alright?" With new vision he evaluated his wife. Her skin was paler than he remembered and there were dark rings under her eyes. Something was definitely wrong.

"I told you, my stomach." A sudden cramp precluded a desire for more explanation.

"It's time for you to go to the doctor." Anticipating a protest, he continued, "I don't care the cost, you can't go on like this."

Lilian finally looked up and into her husband's dark comforting eyes. Tears brimmed and she nodded in surrender.

✶✶✶

"She's actually resting now," Nick cupped his hand around his mouth, trying to soften his voice into his cell phone. "Yes, the kids are here." He paused trying to gage whether to step out into the hallway of the Hospice House for a longer conversation. "I appreciate it."

Lilian smiled, she could tell Nick was trying to end the call. She felt she was in preschool again with the forced "rest" time her family had imposed on her this afternoon. Sure, she was exhausted and probably needed sleep, but her mind never stopped long enough to allow that. She felt as if she was in a vortex, thoughts and questions circling around and around, threatening to suck her into oblivion.

The gnawing pain in her stomach she had attributed to stress turned out to be pancreatic cancer. She replayed the moments leading up to her diagnosis with surreal clarity, paying heed mostly to when the pain started. If I wouldn't have missed my annual exam for four years, would they have caught this earlier? She wondered. Or if I would have gone in the first time I was nauseated, would I be lying here in the Hospice House?

The thoughts tormented her as the 'what if's' piled up like

a traffic jam in her brain. Each question honking its horn, demanding attention.

Amid the swirling thoughts about what could have been, the grand behemoth of all questions anchored itself right in the middle; Why? Why me, why now?

It made her head hurt to contemplate.

Seeing Lilian's brow furrow, Nick, whose phone conversation was over, leaned close and whispered, "Are you hurting? Want me to get the nurse?"

Lilian shook her head. What she longed for was distraction. "When are the kids going to be back?" Her voice was raspy and weak.

Nick looked at his watch, "Any time, they just went to grab lunch."

Lilian willed them to be back, knowing that their humor and conversation would drown out the runaway train of her ruminations.

✶✶✶

Lilian felt a cold sensation shooting up her left forearm. Her eyes flew open to see the Hospice nurse, Angela, standing at the bedside.

"Sorry to wake you, Lilian, I needed to flush this IV before I give you your scheduled medications." Angela was just two years older than her daughter Clarissa, and Lilian wasn't sure if this was comforting or scary.

"What time is it?" Lilian mumbled, surprised to realize she had been sleeping soundly, and more importantly she had slept without thoughts or questions holding her hostage.

"Almost 8 A.M.," Angela announced beaming as if this was

some sort of accomplishment. "I think Dr. Clark will be in shortly, I saw her arrive a bit ago."

Dr. Clark was another young one, Lilian thought, unsure if she trusted her youth. However, in the three days she'd been at the Hospice House, she'd gone from extreme constant hell in terms of vomiting, to just occasional hell. Perhaps the doctor did know what she was doing.

Right on cue, as Angela finished the final push of the nausea and pain medication, the door inched open cautiously and Dr. Audrey Clark peered in.

"Morning," Audrey half whispered with an air of familiarity as she scanned the room for any sleeping family members. Nick was shrouded in blankets, soundly sleeping on the lone couch in the room, but Audrey realized the grown children hadn't spent the night.

"Don't mind him," Lilian spoke, "He would sleep through a freight train coming through the building."

Lilian tried to pull herself up in bed to a half sitting position but struggled to find the strength. Angela quickly jumped in and motioned for Audrey to come help. Both women circled their arms under Lilian's arm pits, as Angela mumbled, "…and three." With ease, they slid Lilian towards the head of the bed and allowed the motorized hospital bed to do the work of supporting Lilian into a sitting position.

"That's much better," Lillian stated, allowing her breathing to slow from the exertion the small move incurred.

Angela slipped out, and Audrey sat in her preferred spot on the edge of Lilian's bed facing her. The two had visited each morning, but Lilian's nausea and pain had limited the ability to talk for very long. Something seemed different that morning, and Lilian found she was eager to speak.

Audrey sensed this, and instead of initiating a string of medical questions, she sat in silence waiting to see what Lilian wanted to discuss.

"Did you know that I almost became a doctor?" Lilian announced with a tinge of pride.

"I did not! There must be a story there."

Lilian's countenance shifted, and she looked over at her husband. "I was accepted into school but made a different decision. I decided to be a mom. Sometimes I wonder..." Lilian let the speculation float away.

Audrey waited for more. Lilian turned her attention back to Audrey and asked, "Do you have children?"

"I do," Audrey answered, "a two-year-old." Audrey's expression communicated the challenge of the age of her daughter. "She's definitely a hand full."

"So, you had her after medical school," concluded Lilian, feeling more at ease with this information.

"Goodness, yes! I'm not sure I would have made it through medical school, let alone residency with a child. Some do, but not me."

An uncomfortable quietness started to develop so Audrey jumped in. "Tell me, Lilian, where are you with all this?" Audrey gestured to the room.

"You mean not being at home?"

"No, I mean having cancer, being on hospice, those things." Audrey hoped she hadn't pressed too hard but felt there was more Lilian was dealing with than just the symptoms of her disease.

Lilian inhaled in an exaggerated way, "Oh," she said as her eyebrows raised, "all of that." Audrey watched Lilian's gaze move to the upper left as she accessed her thoughts.

"To be honest, I've been spending most of my time thinking

about what led to this. Dr. Clark, could I have done something different to not be in this situation? Have you read much on pancreas cancer? Does diet have anything to do with it? Or stress? I have certainly been under stress. I also wondered if maybe I could have exercised more. I kept saying that I was going to join a gym. Who am I kidding! We didn't have money for a membership. What causes cancer anyway?"

Audrey let the tangential questions and thoughts being directed at her shift in her brain trying to decide what her approach should be.

"That sure is a lot of focus on things you can't change."

"Maybe," Lilian considered the observation, "but I'm just trying to figure this out."

"What if I told you, that you can't figure it out? That the why, can never be answered."

Lilian shook her head back and forth, "There has to be something to point a finger at."

"Ah ha, now we get to the real issue," Audrey was pleased Lilian shed some light on what she was struggling with. "You are looking for the cause so that you can place blame somewhere. And it seems from your questions earlier, that you are most comfortable with the blame going to you."

The insight rattled around in Lilian as she tried to find another explanation. The truth was like a needle popping the balloons of all her weak arguments until there was only one thought left, Audrey was right.

"I should tell you," Audrey added, "looking for something or someone to blame is pretty normal. I have some patients who blame the system, some blame other people, but self-blame is by far the most common."

Lilian was at a loss. The idea that she could let go of her own culpability seemed like stepping off into an abyss. What would fill all the space that those questions had occupied in her brain? The unknown was more frightening than the thought patterns that were normal to her. Yet, Lilian was a pleaser, and felt compelled to continue the dialogue, despite having little interest in change.

"What do you suggest I do then, Doctor?" She tried hard not to sound dismissive.

Audrey fiddled a bit, trying to smooth out a wrinkle in the top sheet of Lilian's bed, then said, "I guess I'd say, spend less time analyzing past decisions and try to focus on the present." Audrey ended her speech and scanned Lilian's hazel eyes to see if she was being too direct.

Nick coughed loudly startling both women. His large frame turned to face them, and his eyes opened groggily. As soon as he registered that Audrey was in the room, he sat up quickly with a startled what-did-I-miss look on his face.

Audrey chuckled and began to rise from the bed addressing Lilian again, "Medically your symptoms seem well managed at this point. Would you agree?" Lilian nodded and Audrey continued, "Like we discussed when you were admitted here a few days ago, I'm going to be switching you to residential status now. Nothing changes in your care; it just tells your health insurance company we've gotten things under control."

"Do you think her cancer is slowing down at all?" Nick asked hopefully, "and that maybe we have more time than we thought?"

Audrey grimaced, directing her response at Nick, "I hate to say it, but that's doubtful. Unfortunately, everything else points to continued aggressive growth. Her skin is more jaundiced, and her numbers in key areas are all heading the wrong direction." Audrey turned back to Lilian and asked gently, "You haven't been able to eat anything in over a week, is that right?" Lilian nodded in consent. Audrey let that information speak for itself.

The room door opened, and Lilian's three children strode in, somewhat hesitant when they saw Audrey. Anson led the way into the room with a cardboard drink dispenser full of coffees. The two sisters who followed looked as if they could be twins.

"I was just leaving," Audrey told the grown kids, adding, "Your mom is feeling pretty well today," as she exited the room. Audrey's hunch was that this would be one of Lilian's last really good days and was pleased that all three kids were taking time off school to be at the Hospice House.

"Morning, Mom," Charlotte greeted, coming to give her mom a quick hug. Her straight hair was pulled back in a messy bun, and Lilian worried she looked too thin. A feeling of guilt swept over Lilian, knowing her disease was putting a strain on all of them.

Clarissa spoke, "We just saw the cutest kid out there playing in the kid area. He stopped us to tell us about one of his dinosaurs, the 'T-whex'. It totally reminded me of Anson and his dinosaur phase." Clarissa wrinkled her nose at Anson, who gave a pretend dinosaur roar.

Anson sat the coffees on a small table in the room and addressed his father, "We were just going to bring you a coffee, but," a teasing grin appeared, "since you gave us your credit card, we decided to treat ourselves and the nurses."

Clarissa sank into a seat next to her dad and joined the joke, "We may have also stopped by a particular clothing store that I love, as well." Clarissa's eyes twinkled up at her father, who played his part well showing mock surprise.

Lilian was just going to reprimand her children when Charlotte, who didn't like the teasing, confessed, "Not true. Mom, don't worry, dad did not give us his credit card, and no clothing stores are open this early."

"Char!" Clarissa raised her voice, "You're no fun! Mom can handle a joke; she's the one who taught us the skill!"

Anson spoke up, "Remember the time, mom, you put clear nail polish on our soap bar in the bathroom? I could not figure out why it wasn't sudsing up!" Anson made the motion of washing his forearm and chuckled. "And none of us wanted to say anything, for fear the problem was us, not the soap!"

"So funny!" laughed Clarissa, "or that time you replaced the white cream of our Oreos with white toothpaste. I about threw up! Char, you started crying, you were so mad."

"Of course, I did!" Charlotte argued, "I was only five years old and I thought it meant Oreos would forever taste like pasty mint toothpaste."

The banter and laughter went back and forth as the kids reminisced. Nick laughed the hardest of them all, great big guffaws, as he recalled the antics his wife had fostered for their family. He had missed this. With two away at college, he had forgotten how rambunctious an evening home could get.

Lilian, too, absorbed the exchange with delight. She saw Charlotte wiping tears of laughter from her eyes as she recounted one of her homemade Halloween costumes that Lilian had made.

"To think," Charlotte choked in amusement, "that you somehow thought it was okay that I, that I..." She could hardly speak, she was laughing so hard, "...that I could be a toilet bowl for Halloween."

Anson, too, could barely contain himself, his voice high pitched as he squeezed out the words, "and that you took off our own toilet seat to use, because you didn't want to buy one!"

Lilian let out a snort of laughter and covered her face, "What was I thinking?" Lilian detected her thoughts trying to take her down the familiar road of regrets, lulling her to the past to feel embarrassment. Instead she fought to stay present and allowed herself to take in the scene before her.

Her husband sat on the couch, his arm around Clarissa as she nestled into her father still giggling. Anson stood in the middle of the room, imitating how Charlotte had waddled the year she had dressed as a toilet bowl, his arms held out in a circle symbolic of the round toilet seat. Clarissa sat next to Lillian, doubled over in the hilarity of the imitation.

A deep warm awareness originating in Lilian's chest, spread upward into her shoulders, neck, and face. Could this be the ever-elusive feeling of joy? She wondered. She grinned broadly and let the tears slide down her cheeks. She was overcome with gratitude for her family and her life.

The upsurge of merriment from the others slowly ebbed as they recognized that Lilian was weeping. "Mom, what's wrong?" Charlotte asked fearfully, as she immediately reached for her mother's hand. Concern flashed across Nick's features, as he disentangled himself from Clarissa and came to the bedside.

Lilian shook her head to dispel their apprehension and tried to speak, "Nothing's wrong." Her lip quivered and she wiped the tears off her cheeks. "I'm just so lucky to have you all." Anson and Clarissa had joined Nick and Charlotte encircling the bed. Lilian looked directly at Nick, their gaze tethered, "I haven't been able to realize it until now, but I can finally say with absolute assurance... I made the right choice."

Nick let out a slight sob and leaned over the bed to kiss his wife on the forehead. She felt the lingering moisture from his lips and breathed in his familiar scent, surprised at what she could experience with the distraction of disappointment gone. Nothing more needed to be said, and as each child gave her a hug, she remained hyper alert to every sensation.

They settled back to the places they'd been sitting, Anson breaking the silence with a tease, "Way to make Mom cry, Clarissa, making her feel bad about the toilet bowl!" Clarissa scowled in mock annoyance and the reminiscing revved up again.

7. GOODBYE

Ned

"Papa," five-year-old Cissy called out as she sprinted just out of Ned's reach, "you can't get me!" Cissy's nearly white blonde hair swung from her meticulous pigtails, tempting Ned to give chase, but he was winded from the last three taunts of his granddaughter.

"Cissy, give me a minute to catch my breath." Ned's slender figure bent slightly forward as he rested his hands on his upper thighs trying to slow his breathing.

"C'mon old man," Ned's eldest son, Eli, goaded him, "Surely my daughter hasn't worn you out already." Eli had just stepped out the back door of his parent's home and Cissy bounded her way to him, losing patience in her Papa.

"Flip me, Dad," Cissy commanded, lifting her arms above her

ears in readiness. She turned her head towards her grandfather and added, "This is how you do it, Papa." Eli took Cissy's hands in his and she leaned backwards, using her feet to climb up Eli's legs. Eli kept tension with his grip raising his arms at the end to allow his daughter the ability to flip backwards.

Eli and Cissy chuckled with the success of the flip and Cissy immediately ran to Ned, raising her arms, "Your turn, Papa."

No longer out of breath, Ned felt he must give this a try. He tried to mimic his son's previous moves, allowing Cissy to walk up his legs as he raised her arms higher.   Suddenly there was a pop in Ned's back and searing pain. He instinctively let go of Cissy's hands and dropped to his knees, both hands clutching his lower back. Cissy was only half way through her flip, and at the sudden loss of tension, she dropped forcefully to the ground landing on her back.

Both grandfather and granddaughter cried out simultaneously.   Eli rushed over, on the verge of laughter, until he saw the expression on his father's face. Ned's eyes were closed, eyes squinted, brow furrowed, and Eli thought he saw a tear escape down his father's cheek.

Through gritted teeth Ned whispered, "Help me lie back, I don't want to move myself, and call Prudence out. I think I broke something." Eli's heart pounded, he'd not seen pain like this in his father before. He supported Ned's upper back, gently lowering him to the grass. Cissy's own injury had disappeared, and she came and huddled next to her grandfather, tears already flowing.

"Cis, you stay here with Papa, okay?" Eli vaulted back thru the rear of the house as Cissy's whimpered apologies peppered the stillness.

***

Eli stood outside room 407 at The University of Kansas Hospital, hesitating. The door was closed, and although the nurse on unit 43 told him to go on in, he paused, his feet feeling sluggish and resisting further movement. What would he say to his dad? Eli wondered again if this was all actually real. The sudden collapse the day before had been an unexpected scare; however, that was only the first shock. At the Emergency Room x-rays confirmed crushed vertebra and a broken back that would need emergent surgery to stabilize. It took some time for the family to adjust to the ramifications of such a serious mishap, only to be deluged a short time later with a bigger crisis; the reason Ned's back had broken so easily, was that it was riddled with cancer.

The adjacent door to the room beside Eli opened and a young man stepped out with tears streaming down his face, making a bee line for the exit. An older gentleman followed calling, "Miles, stop, let's talk about this." Feeling awkward at the private moment unfolding, Eli sucked in his fear and pushed open the door to his father's room.

Eli forced a smile as he entered, noting immediately how different his father looked. In the short night away from his parents, Eli was sure his dad had aged a decade. Ned matched his son's put-on smile and ushered him to the bed.

"How are you this morning, Dad?" On the inside Eli panicked, thinking what a dumb question to ask someone just diagnosed with cancer.

His father turned the cheer up a notch and replied, "Doing pretty well. This pain pump they have me on is a wonder. I'll be back chasing grandkids in no time."

"That's great to hear," Eli concluded, looking to his mother for her interpretation of the situation. His mother, Prudence, sat close to Ned, a hand resting on his forearm. Despite spending the night in the cramped little room, she looked ready for a social. Her make-up and hair were done, and she too wore the no-big deal expression on her face.

Eli waited for one of them to dole out more information, but instead uneasy quietness settled. He realized he'd have to be the brave one, and tried to conjure nonchalance as he asked, "What, um, did the, uh, oncologist say this morning? Any updates?"

He was sure he saw a zap of pain cross his mother's face and then disappear. His father answered, "Oh, that, well seems like your old man has some type of kidney cancer. But, not to worry, they are getting me all lined up for treatment. Right, Pru?"

His mother's voice chimed in, "Yes, they want to start right away with both radiation and chemotherapy."

Ned added, "You know what a fighter I am. We are going to kick this cancer's butt!" Ned's eyes sparkled as if he was getting ready to embark on a great adventure. Eli couldn't ignore the despair he was feeling and felt tears begging to be released. Ned noticed his son's struggle and quipped, "Hey, now. No tears here. Not allowed."

Ned's command forced the tears inward and Eli's mind surged with hundreds of questions. Eli longed for more precise information. What stage was the cancer? How long would treatment be? Was it even curable? Instead what squeaked out was, "What else did the Doctor say?"

"Ah, you know, just this and that. Doctor speak mostly. The main thing is I'm going to beat this, you watch." Self-confidence oozed from Ned's pores as he puffed up his chest. The movement must have triggered something, as Ned winced suddenly, gritting his teeth.

Prudence patted her husband's arm, "All this talking is wearing him out." She turned to address Eli and added, "Eli, if you wouldn't mind, we're going to have you call your siblings. Your dad doesn't want to keep telling this whole story over and over."

Eli was eager to help, but hesitated. "Mom, but I hardly know what's going on. They are going to have so many questions, don't you think…"

Ned interrupted, "What's going on is simple. I am going to jump through all the hoops I need and get back to my old self in no time." Ned's tone was dismissive, and Eli understood it was time to go. As he stood, he had the desire to go give his father a hug and tell him how sorry he was that all of this was happening. For an instant he considered doing it, but the hard, unapproachable look on Ned's face drove him away.

✶✶✶

"I'm telling you, Emily, that's all I know." Eli's voice was sterner than he had intended, and as he listened to his younger sister's exasperated questions on the other end of his cell phone, he tried to relax himself. Eli stood alone in his bedroom, purposefully taking the call away from his wife, Adrian, and Cissy. It seemed he had been unofficially deemed the family spokesperson, and fielded phone calls from his four other siblings almost every night.

"But we haven't been up to see him since our Memorial Day family thing, how can he possibly not want us to visit?" Emily was the baby of the five siblings and by far the most dramatic. She and her husband, Beau, lived far enough away that their trips back to Kansas were limited to once or twice a year.

"Emily, listen, I am not the one making this decision. I'm just passing on what Mom said. It's not like they sit around all day with nothing to do. She and Dad are at the hospital, clinic, or treatment center every other day. The days they are home, I think Dad just sleeps."

"I just don't get why they don't want to see us." Emily sounded on the verge of tears now, and Eli shifted his weight in discomfort.

"Then call and ask that. I can't continue to be the go between for this emotional stuff."

The anger came back in a force and a note of bitterness echoed, "I have tried Eli. They won't return my calls. You at least get to be there, see them, talk to them…It's so unfair."

Eli let the statement fizzle into quietness and then softly said, "It is unfair; all of it. It's unfair I have to handle everyone's questions and emotions. But, most of all it's unfair to him. He's dying, Emily, and doesn't realize it." There were muffled cries on the other end and Eli felt guilty for his words. "I'm sorry. It seems none of us is going through this very well." The crying continued, but less ardent. Eli added, "I'll talk to Mom and see if I can push her to find a weekend that we can have everyone come up."

"Thanks," was the subdued response, and then almost inaudibly, "I'm sorry, too."

★★★

Eli walked the path up to his childhood home, stooping to pick up three missed newspapers strewn about the yard. He intentionally pushed down any nostalgic thoughts that tried to sprout up, knowing that his father wouldn't accept what he deemed 'mushy sentimentalism'. He knocked quietly and could hear his mother walking to the door. They were expecting him; otherwise, they would likely not have opened the door.

Prudence looked spotless in her appearance; though, Eli could tell she was requiring more make-up than usual to keep that facade.

"Eli," his mother greeted, "your father's in the den." Prudence turned in the opposite direction, dismissing any chance to talk directly to her.

Eli took the short five steps down into the den and found his father stretched out on his leather recliner with his eyes closed. A large family quilt covered Ned's body, and a well-worn T.V. tray was placed nearby littered with facial tissues, two remotes, a glass of water and multiple pill bottles. Eli took a moment to mine his father's appearance for clues of his condition.

In the six weeks of intense treatments, Ned had lost over 30 pounds. His skin sagged from his upper arms and neck. The color of his skin was pale, and the aging process seemed to have accelerated even more. Eli cleared his throat attempting to gently awaken his father.

Ned's eyes snapped open, a slight flush of embarrassment that he'd been caught sleeping appeared momentarily, and then he composed himself.

"Good morning, son. I can't imagine why you wanted to spend your Saturday coming to visit me, but your mother insisted. What's on your mind?" Ned's voice was not as robust as Eli was used to, but still as commanding as ever.

Eli took a seat in the matching recliner and leaned forward towards his father. "I really was just hoping for an update. I know you met again with the oncologist this past week, and, well to be honest, all of us feel in the dark about what's happening."

Ned nodded in understanding, his brow slightly furrowed.

"Frankly, I'm not sure what there is to be in the dark about. But the update is this; we are moving to a different chemotherapy this next week. It's more powerful, and my understanding is it is harder on the body." Ned pulled out his salesman face, the one Eli had grown up seeing when his father practiced different sales pitches on the family, "I told the doctor to do whatever it takes to beat this thing. He was hesitant to move to this drug, but I convinced him I could take it." A hint of pride seasoned his words and he smiled.

Eli looked baffled, "Is the other treatment already done? I thought it was supposed to be given for several months?"

Ned batted down the question with his hand, swiping it away. "It wasn't working as well as they wanted," Ned shrugged his shoulders, "So, it's time to move on."

It was Eli's turn to nod, he was trying to process this information quickly and infer reality in the midst of his father's narrative.

There was a shuffle of someone on the steps and Eli turned to see his mother coming down the stairs with a tall glass of thick bright orange liquid.

"What is that?" Eli asked with disgust.

His father chuckled, "My breakfast; 100% raw vegetables. Not the easiest to get down, but who said fighting cancer was easy."

Prudence handed off the concoction and took a seat on the couch opposite the men. "We read about this on the internet. People are cured of cancer all the time drinking this." Prudence beamed at Eli.

Skeptical, Eli asked, "What's in it? It's so bright it almost glows!"

Prudence named off the ingredients on her fingers, "carrots, beets, cabbage, broccoli and cauliflower." She looked up and added, "And of course the powder medicine."

Eli frowned, "What powder medicine?"

"I think it's called Cellcure. It's been shown to cure cancer; it's something we bought online."

Eli turned from his mother, back to his father and then back to his mother again, looking for signs of a practical joke. "How much does this cancer cure cost?" Eli tried hard to keep his voice level, but inside was reeling with the stupidity of the idea.

His father looked slightly sheepish as he answered, "I think we calculated the Cellcure out at $50."

Eli sighed in relief, "Oh, $50 dollars a month, that's not bad at all. Of course, all those fresh veggies have to be expensive."

Prudence interrupted, "No dear, $50 a dose. Three times a day."

Eli's eyes nearly popped from their sockets and he sputtered in reaction. His father interceded quickly, "I know it seems like a lot, but it's nothing compared to how much chemotherapy costs, and really, is there any price too high for a cure?"

Eli shook his head, still reeling from this information. He wanted to argue that insurance would be covering most of the chemotherapy, and that they didn't have the extra income to pour down the drain of false hope. Instead he buttoned his lips and took a deep breath. There was no sense in arguing. He decided to switch topics.

"There was something else I wanted to ask you both about."

Prudence looked weary at the possibility of hard conversation but answered anyway, "Go on."

"Emily, Chad, Emerson, and Darrin all want to find a weekend to come visit." Immediately a spark of tension ignited, and Eli held his hand up to ward off the arguments, "No wait, listen, they have the right to come see you both. They are all worried, and I am tired of babysitting them on the phone. If you make it one weekend, then you can get it over with. Otherwise, I'm telling you they will start coming one by one and you'll never have a break."

Ned looked toward the ceiling in disgust, "So much drama and hubbub. Can't I just be left to recover on my own? Once I'm back up on my feet, then we can have a big celebration. I don't need a bunch of kids running around and questions every few minutes about how I am doing!"

Eli was stern in his response, "I hear you. But it can't always be about you. You might not need them here, but they need to see you." Eli felt sick speaking to his father like this, but the days of coaxing his siblings to calm down and respect their dad's wishes had taken their toll.

Anger clouded Ned's expression, his jaw tightened, and eyes narrowed. "I see," is all he said, turning his gaze to nothingness across the room.

Prudence wiggled on the couch, clearly uncomfortable with the tension. Eli turned towards her, pleading with his eyes for her to side with him. She lowered her gaze, willing herself to escape. Finding this to be the only reality available, she inhaled, met Eli's stare and conceded. "I'll look at the calendar later and find a weekend." She glanced at her husband who still was avoiding the conversation. She added, "The one stipulation is that no one can stay here... and we will set some specific times for them to visit during the day."

Ned's sour expression faded slightly, but he still refused to rejoin the dialogue. Eli knew he was being dismissed, so he rose and faced his father. The same compelling feeling of wanting to embrace this stubborn man surged, but once again Eli stuffed the impression away. His teeth clenched with the resolve not to get emotional and he turned to leave. Over his shoulder on his way out, fighting composure he was able to squeeze out, "Thank you."

★★★

Eli's basement was chaos. Eleven cousins, ages nine and under ran rampant, energized by too much sugar and little parental supervision. The adult siblings and significant others had escaped into the kitchen and living room, pretending to ignore the occasional crashing sounds from below.

The mood was heavy as the group digested the latest condition to their planned visit over at their parent's home, later that afternoon.

"Did she say if the grandkids would be able to see him tomorrow, or not at all?" Emily's voice spewed irritation into the air.

"She only spoke about this afternoon, but I wouldn't put it past them to say no to tomorrow as well." Eli didn't have the heart to let on that he had guessed as much. In the three weeks since he had gotten his mother to concede to a family visit, Ned had become even more closed off.

Chad, the second oldest spoke, "Doesn't he realize we've traveled great distances and some of us have had to take off work to be here?" Resentment resonated in the room, as they all naturally directed their ire towards Eli.

"Hey," He responded defensively, "this isn't my call. I'm just delivering Mom's message." Under his breath he added, "Now you know what I've been dealing with."

The middle son, Emerson caught the words. "What did you say? You don't think it's been hard on our end dealing with this?"

Eli put both hands up protectively.

The youngest of the boys, Darrin, jumped in, "You've at least had the chance to see him, talk to him. We've gotten nothing; ignored like we didn't exist!"

"I'm just frustrated, like all of you. I'm sorry. This isn't exactly how I thought this would go."

The statement helped mollify the room and Emily rose from her seat at the kitchen table to go refill her coffee, speaking as she walked. "I think you've nailed it Eli, this isn't proceeding how any of us thought." Several nodded and Emily continued, stirring creamer into her coffee as she spoke, "When Beau's dad died two years ago, we basically lived at his folk's house." Emily turned and leaned her back against the counter, searching out her husband's face. He nodded encouragingly, and she shared the experience.

"We spent hours laughing and hearing about things from his life. We had time to cry together and tell him goodbye." Tears ran down Emily's cheeks as she recalled the experience. "He even wrote out these precious cards to each of his kids, imparting wisdom and love." Beau wiped the moisture from his eyes but didn't speak.

The room was noiseless for a time, but then Chad's wife, Leah, broke the silence. She too had been crying and was hesitant with her words. "You all know my Mom was killed in a car accident when I was 12." There was general consent around the room, so she resumed, "I just wanted to say, that at least you all have a chance to say goodbye." With those words, Leah pinched the bridge of her nose trying to keep any more tears at bay.

"You're right, Leah," Emerson said remorsefully, "You have a good point."

Darrin, however, was still edgy, "Right, a good point." There was sarcasm in his words, and he concluded, "Yet having the chance to say goodbye and actually getting an opportunity to do so, are two different things." With that, Darrin got up and exited out the front door.

Before anyone else could pipe in, a whining non-descript, "Mom, the boys are being mean," came wafting up the stairs. The moms all glanced at one another hoping someone would claim ownership, but were spared the task when Eli stated, "I've got it," and took off to play referee.

The visit had been shocking for most of the siblings and they found themselves in a bit of a stupor back at Eli's house later that evening. Their father had not wanted any one-on-one time, but instead to have all the adults in to see him all at once. He'd put on a good show, explaining that he was doing well. He chided anyone who portrayed worry or concern and avoided any questions of a serious nature. Most offensive, was the alarm chime that sounded after thirty minutes, declaring the visit over.

Leah and Emerson's girlfriend, Triston, had taken nine of the cousins back to the hotel to be put to bed after graciously watching the kids while the others visited Ned and Prudence. The remaining adults sat in the living room with drinks, digesting the situation.

Emily, the only one standing, rocked her seven-month-old trying to get him to fall asleep and as per usual had much to say. "Do you really think he has a chance at being cured?"

Emerson answered, "Doubtful. Just look at him. He looks like he's close to dying as it is."

Chad chimed in, "But to hear him speak, he's just one step away from being cancer free."

Emily asked, "Do you think the doctors haven't told him, or he's just in denial?"

"I'm guessing it's all him." Eli concluded. "But I'll find out soon. I'm going with him and Mom to his next appointment this Tuesday. They tried to persuade me otherwise, but I'm sick of all this nebulous talk."

This information pleased everyone. Darrin said, "You better ask that doctor how much time Dad's got left." As an after-thought he added, "… and maybe see if he can give Dad some kind of happy pill."

Emerson smiled at this, "No joke, he was grumpy!"

Chad turned to Emily, "Did he actually call you a blubbering baby?"

Emily rolled her eyes, but it was easy to see the hurt that lingered at her father's name calling.

Adrian, who had spent most of her time hosting all her in-laws, decided she'd add in her two-cents. "I'll tell you what worries me: Prudence. She looks unhealthy herself. How much work is she doing each day, each hour, to take care of him?"

None of the siblings had considered this problem, but it clearly bothered them.

"Ask about that too," Darrin declared.

Eli raised one eyebrow and smirked, "If she'll let me."

＊＊＊

Emily was the last one on Eli's list to call with an update. He was bone weary, but didn't have the luxury of collapsing into bed, as much as his body craved the idea. The visit with the oncologist had been serendipitous, and Eli tried not to surmise what would have happened had he not been there.

Eli was astonished at the picture Dr. Brandenberry presented of Ned's condition. Ned had a failed response to all the treatments they had tried, including something called 'salvage therapy' which sounded bad in and of itself. For the first time in the process, Eli heard the name of the cancer; Renal Cell Carcinoma, as well as the staging; stage IV.

He shuddered when he realized that treatment was never about a cure, only about prolonging his father's life. At least a dozen times, Eli had looked over at his father, trying to grasp the delusion they'd all been showered with. But looking at his father's expression of determination, he understood that his father had put up some mental barrier against reality. Even there in the office, Eli could envision the doctor's words bouncing off his father's exterior.

The doctor was saying there was nothing left to do, and yet Ned smiled on, and though he needed help standing and an arm to support him walking, he departed saying, "I'm sure I'll be stronger the next time I see you."

In desperation, Eli had quickly motioned to speak to the doctor alone and allowed his parents to slowly make their way out, while lingering behind.

That's when the final blow came. Eli learned that the doctor thought Ned may only have weeks left to live.

"I'm glad you came today," Dr. Brandenberry had said, "I've been worried about your father, but also your mother. I think she needs help, this is too much for her to do alone." Eli had agreed wholeheartedly but didn't know what to do. Dr. Brandenberry suggested that Eli should persuade his mother to allow hospice to come into the home. "Explain that it would be for her, and that she wouldn't even need to let on that it was hospice. Call it visiting nurses."

Astonishingly Eli had convinced his mother of the scheme, and the nurse had agreed to meet them the following morning.

Emily eventually answered the phone, breathless and with a note of panic in her voice. He guessed like himself, any phone call from family these days was etched in fear of what news the caller would bring.

Eli's tone was purposefully calm, "I finally have quite a bit of information for you, and you may want to sit down for this."

✱✱✱

Eli waited patiently in the den at his parent's house for the hospice nurse, Tami, to finish her visit with Ned. His stomach was in knots, wondering if his father would be as rude to Tami as he was on her first visit. He was having a hard time reconciling this angry and bitter man with the father he knew. Was it just three months ago that Ned was chasing Cissy around the back-yard? The thought took his breath away.

Tami entered the den cautiously, not wanting to interrupt Eli's thoughts unexpectedly. Eli had only met Tami once before but was impressed with her nurturing way.

"Did he send you packing?" Eli asked.

Tami sat opposite and her expression was warm. "He would have liked to, I'm sure." They both chuckled. "You know, Eli, what I see in your dad, is someone who is extremely scared."

Eli looked perplexed. "He must have changed personalities again, because all I've seen is a closed off, angry man, not someone quaking in their boots."

The image made both of them smile, and Tami explained, "That's one way I suppose of showing fear. But another way is denial."

"I agree with the denial part. Before you got here, he told me that later today he wanted me to help him get some exercise. He literally said 'can't let my muscles get too weak or I'll never be able to beat this.' Are you kidding me? He can't even sit up in bed without one of us helping him." Tami nodded like she wasn't surprised. Eli continued, "Then, when I told him that exercise was impossible and pointed out how weak he was, he blew a gasket."

"You know why that is, right?" Eli shrugged his shoulders, wishing he knew why the man, who never lost his temper growing up, was suddenly having his fuse tripped a dozen times a day. Tami continued, "You were contradicting his reality."

"Huh?"

"He's spent the last months building a house of cards around the illusion he would be cured. Anything that challenges his delusion could knock down those cards. Talk about terrifying."

Tami looked at her watch, "I'm sorry, I have to go, but I'll be back in two days. Some of your siblings will be here then, right?"

Eli rolled his eyes while nodding yes, thinking about what his father's reaction to the surprise visit from the family would be.

Responding to Eli's expression, Tami quipped, "You're insinuating that I need to be prepared, huh?"

Eli allowed a grin to spread across his face as he enjoyed the banter. "Let's just say there could be some actual explosions."

★★★

"This is so wrong! I hate this pretending," hissed Darrin through gritted teeth. He was getting ready to enter Ned's bedroom with Chad. Prudence was the gatekeeper, allowing only two in at a time, and for a few minutes only.

"Eli said we had to, and it's for Dad's sake, not ours," Chad argued back.

Darrin moved to open the door and as he walked into the room he whispered, "Well, it makes me want to vomit."

The queen-sized bed in the room had been pushed to the side to allow for a hospital bed in the room. And a few extra chairs were present. It was cluttered and crowded, and both boys sidestepped furniture to make it to the bed. Tami had explained to the family that Ned's kidneys were obstructed, and that urine was building up in his system. She had told them she guessed it would be painless, with his kidney's failing, and that he'd essentially go to sleep and into a coma.

Prudence was seated by Ned's side and patted his arm to wake him. He was gaunt, pale, and drowsy, but still coherent when awake.

He seemed a bit annoyed to see two of his boys at the foot of his bed. "What are you boys doing here? Come to gawk at your old man?" His tone was gruff, and he continued, "I told Pru, until I was feeling better, there was no need to have visitors."

Chad chimed in with the charade they had rehearsed, "We're not here for you, Dad, Eli's planned a big surprise party for Adrian's 40th birthday. We just thought since we were in town, we'd stop by to say hi, see the progress you're making."

Darrin snorted and Chad elbowed him in the ribs. "Uh, right, you're looking good, Dad," Darrin choked out.

Ned's harsh stance melted with these words, and he smiled. "In that case, I'm glad you stopped by." Chad noticed his mother's eyes were moist. He watched her subtly swallow her tears and refocus. Ned continued, "I was just telling your mother that for Christmas this year we should go somewhere warm and have all you kids join us. I'm sure I'll be ready to travel by then."

Chad nodded agreeably adding, "That's a great idea." Darrin tried to nod but felt a rush of emotion cascading from within. He coughed, trying to hide the reaction, but was overcome. He spun and walked briskly out the door collapsing to the floor outside the bedroom.

He buried his head into his knees and wept.

The siblings were huddled in the den, some in silence, some quietly whimpering. It was 2 A.M. and the group looked disheveled and unkempt. It had been a horrendous few days, as Ned transitioned from lucid but drowsy, to a restless agitator. He had thrashed and kicked sheets off the bed, tried to get up and clawed at the air. He had shouted for help and complained about being held hostage. They had medicated and medicated, but still it escalated. No one had really slept. Tami had tried to explain that he struggled because of the denial, that physically as his body shut down, he raged against it in the same way he'd raged against his family.

Then on a dime, in just a matter of minutes, it had changed. His muscles had relaxed, but he was no longer responsive. A strange purple color had appeared on his legs and his breathing became harsh. Eli called Tami, but before she even arrived, Ned was gone.

They were in shock and undone.

Tami led Prudence down the den stairs, Emily shifting to give their mother a seat on the couch. Tami knelt on the floor, having officially pronounced the death. There was more than disbelief and grief in the room, Tami felt disappointment present as well. She made the decision to address it. "Some of you may be struggling right now, because you didn't have a chance to say goodbye."

Emily let out a sob, and Emerson snapped his head towards Tami, surprised she had put a name to his irritation.

Tami continued, "Even if you had been given more time, I'm not sure Ned would ever have accepted a goodbye." Darrin looked up now, his eyes narrowing. Tami continued, "In fact, now may be the best time for goodbyes." A few began to look around at each other confused. Tami caught this and explained, "Not here," she pointed to the den and then lifted her finger towards the rooms above, "with him. The funeral home won't be here for about an hour, so there is time."

No one moved initially. Eli looked around the room and felt the familiar longing to embrace his father surge within. He struggled with forcing it back into some internal box but realized this was it; his only chance. Tentatively he rose, a bit squeamish to go back into the room. Each step seemed to break lose his controlled emotions and by the time he reached the bedroom door he was bawling. Finally, he would get to say all he had wanted to say.

8. VALOR

Frank

Frank tried hard to suppress the cough, because he knew that if he gave into the urge, his chest would burn with rippling spasms of pain throughout his torso, and he would not be able to quit coughing until he nearly passed out. Instead, he forced out a small moan, trying to appease the tickle in his windpipe.

"Dad, are you hurting? Do you need me to call for the nurse?" asked Ron, overly attentive to every sound Frank made. Ron, at 62, was the younger version of Frank; tall, lean, a bit gangly, yet distinguished looking.

Frank shook his head no but did not want to speak for fear it would trigger the cough. He sat hunched forward in the room's recliner, his right forearm bearing his weight across the top of his knee. His left arm, which had been amputated just above the elbow joint, hung close to his side but provided no support.

As the urge to cough passed, his muscles relaxed and he sat back gingerly in the chair. "I'm fine, Ron, just trying not to cough. I can't seem to remember a time when I wasn't coughing." Frank gave Ron a half smile, recalling exactly when the cough had started. It was four months ago and he had been celebrating his 88th birthday at home. All three of his grown children and their families had been able to come. The kids had felt bad for him, he supposed, his first birthday alone after he lost his beloved wife Jean.

Mark, their youngest, had insisted that Frank have a cake with candles, and when he took a deep breath to blow them out, it had triggered a coughing fit. Brenda, their only daughter, had patted him on the back teasing him about being an 'old man'. The cough never really went away after that June celebration. It was not until he coughed up blood a few weeks ago, that he went to see a doctor.

Was he really surprised, he wondered, when the x-ray had shown a mass in the middle left lobe of his lung? No. He had known something was wrong; he had lost 20 lbs. in two months, and was taking frequent naps, which was so unlike him. What had surprised him, though, was that the cancer seemed to be everywhere. That, and how the oncologist had counseled him to enroll in hospice, saying his time was very limited.

A week later and here he was, living residentially at the Hospice House.

Ron, on the other hand, hadn't seen any of it coming. He was shocked when his father called, sharing the devastating news. Frank had always been the epitome of industrious, independent manhood. He was never sick, never needed assistance with anything, and expected the same from those around him. Ron recalled the time at the age of six when he broke his arm falling out of the giant oak tree in their yard. It was a warm summer night, and he and his brother were playing after supper. Ron had hollered out in pain, and lay on the ground writhing, as Mark ran to get their parents. Frank stepped onto the porch and crossed his arms, a look of disappointment across his face. Jean stood timidly behind him, a worried look in her eyes. Ron continued to sob, which made Frank's face flush. Frank spoke sternly, "Ronald James, you will get off that ground and stop crying like a baby. Hansen men do not act like this!"

Ron had immediately quieted himself to a whimper and pushed himself up. Ron's arm hung at an abnormal angle, yet his father did not budge from his rigid stance. Ron learned that day that no injury, emotional or physical, warranted tears.

Despite Frank's efforts, he was suddenly caught off guard by a tickle in his throat and allowed a cough to escape which triggered the cascade of searing pain and nausea. He gasped for breath, as his upper body shook violently.

Angela, Frank's nurse, hearing the fit, walked briskly into the room and over to Frank. Ron was on his feet, already at his father's side, a look of concern on his face as he watched his father struggle. The event ended, with Frank, once again, leaning forward, panting and sweating as if he had just finished running.

"Frank," inquired Angela, "will you let me bring you something for your cough? The doctor ordered morphine, which really is helpful for coughing." Frank, still catching his breath, shook his head emphatically no.

"Dad, why won't you take something? You are miserable!" Ron pleaded, while Frank continued to shake his head no. Ron locked eyes with Angela, his expression a mix of embarrassment and annoyance at his father's refusal.

Sympathetically, Angela reassured both of them, "It's okay. Please know, Frank, we have many options of medicines that can help you, so you do not need to suffer." Angela walked to Frank's bedside table and lifted his water pitcher to assess how full it was and asked, "Would you like me to help you get into your bed so you can rest some this morning?"

Frank immediately sat up straighter in his chair and answered, "No thank you. I am very comfortable where I am."

Ron and Angela again exchanged looks, this time the nurse shrugged her shoulders at Ron, as if to say, we tried. With Frank refusing most of her suggestions, Angela excused herself. As soon as she stepped out into the hallway, she spotted Dr. Audrey Clark entering the nurse's unit and made a beeline for her.

"Morning, Angela" said Audrey, the thirty-something year old physician, currently assigned to the Hospice House. She wore her stethoscope draped around her neck, and her trademark unruly short hair framed her warm smile. "They called me at 3 a.m. about Scott passing. Do you know if his wife ever made it up here?"

Angela rolled her eyes as she responded with a no. She normally would have enjoyed talking to Dr. Clark about the dysfunction of family members, but she had more pressing issues like Frank to deal with. "Can I update you on Frank first?"

"Sure. Tell me what is going on."

"He has been here three days and has refused to take anything for pain or breathing. He clearly needs something, though. Do you think you can talk to him about it?"

"Absolutely. Is there anything else I should know before going into the room?"

"Well, I don't know if it's related, but he also is refusing to get into his bed. He's sat and slept in that recliner for three days."

Angela's voice rose, unable to disguise her frustration. "Also, I noticed yesterday, when his son was gone, he was in the room talking to himself. He was very tired, but refused to take a nap, just talked and talked to nobody."

"Hmm, interesting, and, yes, it could be related. When someone avoids sleep like that, it can indicate a fear of dying. I'll see if I can get to the bottom of it." Audrey sounded chipper at the challenge before her.

Inside the room, it was cheery. The window blinds were open, allowing maximal light in. The family had placed photos on every available surface top. In the center of one such batch of photos was a prominent boxed frame. Inside the frame was a heart-shaped medal with a golden surface attached to a purple ribbon.

"Good morning, Frank," Audrey greeted her patient cheerfully and approached his recliner, "Do you mind if I sit on your bed and visit?" Her kindness elicited a smile from Frank, as he turned his body towards the doctor and nodded affirmatively. "Tell me how you are feeling this morning."

"I am doing pretty well, considering," Frank answered stoically. "This cough is kicking my butt, but otherwise, nothing to complain about." Ron, who had been working on a laptop, set it aside, eager to see what Dr. Clark would do or say.

"About that cough, and your breathing, which I can tell is difficult even sitting here, why haven't you wanted to take any medicine to help alleviate your symptoms?"

"I don't need that crap," Frank said grinning, seeing if Audrey would react. Audrey smiled back at this gentle man who was deflecting the deeper question and decided to try a different approach. She was aware that she had Ron's full attention; Ron was obviously concerned about his father.

"I don't know about that, but we won't force anything." She paused trying to decide how to frame the next question. "Frank, the nurses mentioned to me today that you haven't actually gotten into this bed to sleep since you've arrived." Audrey left space for Frank to jump in, when he simply nodded, she pressed harder. "I've had patients before who didn't want to get into bed, and do you know what many of them told me?" Audrey could see Frank was interested, "They told me that they were afraid. They worried that if they fell asleep, they would die. The beds symbolized sleep, and sleep symbolized death, and they were not ready to die." Audrey hoped by normalizing her hunch, Frank would verbalize his reasons for avoiding sleep.

Frank's countenance changed immediately, as emotion billowed up within him. He felt somewhere internally a wall was crumbling. He had spent most of his adult life stuffing emotions, but this illness had taken the fight out of him, and he did not have the strength to hold back the past any longer. In a somewhat defeated way and on the verge of tears, Frank said, "Yes. You are right. I am afraid." A sob escaped from Frank, despite the effort to remain controlled. Ron's eyes grew large in surprise and he sat forward in his chair. Audrey congratulated herself internally for guessing correctly.

Frank continued, but now large crocodile tears dripped from his eyes, "But not afraid of dying." Here a few more sad wails came forth, as Audrey knit her brows in confusion. "I am afraid of dying a cowardly death," he concluded with shame besieging the statement.

The emotion and the statement caught Audrey off guard, and she was not sure what Frank meant. Clearly, this was something big. She leaned closer and placed her hand on Frank's forearm and asked encouragingly, "Can you explain that to me, Frank?

What does that mean, a cowardly death?"

Frank sighed, his shoulders heaving now with silent sobs. It would feel good finally to talk about it, so he decided to dive in. "I'm going to tell you a story." The memory played in his mind vividly as he narrated his experience.

"It was March 1945. The Allies had not only survived, but we had won the Battle of the Bulge and were pushing East across the Rhine River. I was a sergeant in the 395th regiment of the 99th infantry.

It was still cool in Germany, and everything was bare and muddy from the melted snow. On March 15th, I was leading my platoon of 12 men, advancing our line. We were pinned down by heavy machine gun and mortar fire from a German nest in a wooded area ahead.

Suddenly, out of the corner of my eye, I saw an explosion and heard my buddy Mac scream. His screaming triggered something within me, and in a rage of anger, without even thinking, I set off directly towards the enemy gunfire. I heard this animalistic cry as I ran towards the shell hole, readying my grenades. I didn't know it at the time, but it was actually me who was screaming out like a banshee. I climbed up the embankment of the hole, slipping a bit in the mud, and with all my might threw the two grenades in either hand. Immediately, the double explosion knocked me to the ground, and there was a terrible pain in my left side. I was still operating on adrenaline, though, and ran back to Mac's position and called for a Medic. Mortar shells continued to blast all around, and finally one of those explosions jolted me back to reality. I recall feeling woozy, and had a hard time thinking clearly. I do remember scanning the area and seeing the bodies of my platoon members and being overcome with grief as darkness swept over me.

When I came to, it took me time to realize that I was in a field tent hospital. The smell of antiseptic and burned flesh assaulted my senses. My pain was coming from my left side, and when I looked, I saw my left arm wrapped in bandages. Something was seeping through them, making me avert my eyes. I could sense more burns on my left leg and side. It was like I was being stuck with thousands of hot needles. I heard, then, an agonizing cry and carefully turned my head towards the cot on my right. The man there looked like a mummy, completely covered with bandages. I knew in that instant, however, that this was Mac. He moaned again, and I called out, 'Mac, it's me, Frank. You made it out!'

Mac responded proudly, 'That's right.' Then he added more somberly, 'You and I both did, though they tell me we are the only two from the platoon alive.' I could tell Mac was in pain by the way his body jerked and grew tense. I'd guess 80% of his body was burned. As I watched him fighting the pain, he gritted his teeth and said to me, 'You SOB, you better promise me that you'll be here come morning.'"

At this Frank stopped his story, finding it hard to speak, lost in the memory. Audrey and Ron sat riveted on Frank's every word. After a few more tears, Frank continued.

"I answered him back, 'I promise, but Mac, you better promise too, don't you leave me.' Mac let out another anguished cry, and then half yelled, 'we'll fight!'

I didn't sleep much that night. It was hard to rest with all the commotion from the nurses coming in and out, and the sounds of other soldiers calling out in pain. I was aware of Mac all that night, hearing his tormented moans and piercing cries. I must have eventually dozed off soundly, for when I woke up there was this beautiful ambient light from the sunrise projecting through the tent walls. I sensed movement on my right side, which I'm guessing is what woke me. It came to me quickly; I hadn't heard Mac's voice in a while. I turned to his cot, fearing what my brain was already telling me. There I saw a nurse pulling up the sheet over Mac's head, as another attendant removed the stethoscope that had just confirmed that Mac was gone. He had hung on until first light."

As Frank ended the summary of this vivid experience to Audrey and his son, his tears slowed. A respectful silence followed. Audrey felt as if a gear had shifted into its proper place somewhere inside her. Of course Frank feared an easy painless death, she thought, his formative understanding of dying had been to endure all suffering and fight to live until the last shred of life was severed.

With new understanding, Audrey broke the silence. "What a privilege to understand your perspective, Frank. To clarify, taking morphine to ease your pain, or help you breathe better, and physically getting in bed to relax and sleep, you fear is not being courageous?"

Frank silently sobbed and nodded affirmatively, adding, "Death isn't meant to be easy."

Ron jumped into the conversation, his voice filled with compassion. "Dad, this is the first time I've heard any story at all about the war. I had no idea…" His speech trailed off.

Frank's crying began anew, "There is so much to say." He looked up, directly into Ron's eyes, "So much that haunts me." Ron at this point stood and moved his chair close to his father. Frank turned and looked at Audrey, unable to say his next words to his son. "We knew in theoretical terms that we killed people, but occasionally you directly witnessed the enemy die by your own hand." Frank paused and wiped his dripping nose with a handkerchief from nearby. His voice became high pitched as he talked through the emotion. It took great effort getting the words out, "I killed three Germans. I can see their faces still, each one, before I shot them." Ron reached his arm out around his father's shoulder to comfort him as Frank wept at this confession.

Something mighty had been released inside Frank, and he continued, "I know I was too hard on you kids. I was stern and had high expectations and kept myself at a distance. I regret that now."

At this, he did look at Ron, searching Ron's face for forgiveness. Ron's loving expression was a relief and Ron responded, "C'mon, you were a great Dad."

Frank went on, "You see, after Mac died, I was sent to a hospital in Belgium for my amputation and to recover. Before my release, General Patton came to award the purple heart to myself and four other injured soldiers. There at the hospital he met with us, congratulated us, and told us how important we had been to the cause. His final words are seared in my brain. He said, 'Remember, the first time you ask for help, you've lost.'"

Frank let out a sad moan and tears fell as he said, "…and I never did ask for help."

Audrey felt a great compassion for Frank and wasn't surprised at the message he had received; the message that strength was equated with self-sufficiency. She longed to bring him comfort. "Frank, I need to tell you something."

Audrey waited for Frank to settle a bit and turn his attention back to the moment. "First, I am sorry that you were told never to ask for help. That for some reason, it was implied that needing help was somehow weak. Second, what you have done just now is one of the most courageous things anyone can do. I see before me a very brave man, someone strong enough to show emotion and strong enough to relive horrific things." Frank and Ron were both crying now, and Audrey felt herself on the verge of tears. "Finally, the way someone exits this world, is not a reflection of who they are and who they have been. You are strong. You are courageous. There is nothing cowardly about you. If you happen to die in your sleep, peacefully, that fact takes nothing away from the life you have lived."

Frank could not respond with words but smiled gratefully at Audrey. Ron quietly said, "Thank you."

Audrey knew it was time to leave, she had more patients to see, yet a strong part of her wanted to linger and be a part of Frank's catharsis. She sighed and shifted her position in the seat, "Well, I must go now. You both have much to talk about and digest, I'm sure." She left the room keenly aware of how rare that conversation had been.

✶✶✶

Angela caught Audrey early again the next morning. As soon as Audrey had set foot into the nurses' station she probed, "Dr. Clark, what did you say to Frank yesterday?"

"We talked about many things, why?" Audrey said as she cocked her head in an inquisitive way.

"He agreed to sleep in his bed last night!" Angela announced triumphantly, adding, "And, he's even taken some doses of morphine for his cough."

Satisfaction spread through Audrey, though she wanted to know more, "I'm glad for that, but Angela, how did he sleep, and how is he feeling?"

"He slept, I mean, really slept, deeply. He spent the rest of the day talking about stories from the War. All of his kids now have been here, and they are just enthralled with all of the anecdotes." Angela's excited tone shifted a bit, "He's also showing signs of changes, though. I think he might be transitioning." Audrey was not surprised to hear this and had guessed that once Frank came to terms with dying that things would start to accelerate.

Audrey looked over Frank's vitals and medication use over the last 24 hours before heading in to talk with him.

The room was still bright, but the atmosphere was altered. Frank looked different in the hospital bed. He was more at peace and not struggling, and yet, there seemed to be less of him now. Frank's three children sat around the room, looking exhausted. His daughter, Brenda, appeared the most frazzled, mascara marks under her puffy eyes from crying. Frank, whose eyes had been shut when Audrey entered, opened them as she drew near. A large grin formed on his face and then tears.

"Morning, Doc. You'll have to forgive the tears. I cannot seem to stop crying. I suppose I am making up for decades of not crying." Frank tried to wink.

Mark chimed in, "This is a completely different dad than what we are used to, but we like it!"

"Look at you in bed! How did you sleep?" Audrey squatted by the head of the bed to be level with Frank's gaze.

"Good, I think." Frank's tears rolled down his face as he admitted, "I'm ready to go now. I actually hoped I might not be here this morning." Audrey glanced over at the family. She was relieved to see not just sadness, but acceptance on their faces. Frank continued, "This might sound odd, but sometime in the night I saw heaven." Frank became more emotional, "I could see Jean and my parents." At this he stopped, there was such grief in his voice now, and longing. "I wanted to go to them, but there was something in the way. It was blocking me, and I didn't know how to get around it."

Ron spoke as a parent would to a child, reassuringly, "Dad, it was just a dream. It's okay."

Audrey jumped in, "Maybe so, but at the end of life, some pretty unbelievable stuff seems to happen." Audrey did not want to discount Frank's experience, "Frank, it sounds to me like you are close. I'm not sure what that barrier represents. It may be something physical you don't have control over." Frank felt reassured by her words. Audrey stood to go, adding, "You did tremendous work yesterday, so few are able to do that." Frank lifted his right hand inviting Audrey to shake it. She grasped his lanky hand with both of hers and squeezed. There was a knowingness that passed between them, that this was goodbye.

Audrey left, with a nod to Frank's grown children. She paused outside the door to collect herself. She thought about the ancient Greek concept of *Kalos Thanatos*, or a beautiful death, ascribed to warriors who died in battle. Though Frank would hopefully die peacefully, his valor certainly epitomized for Audrey what was meant by a beautiful death.

9. IRISH LAMENT

Katherine

"Katherine, eat your breakfast," John chided his wife of 50 years, shuffling up to her armchair. Katherine gently looked into her husband's eyes as he lectured that without enough calories, the human body could not operate properly. He rattled off a plethora of facts and motivational reasons, working the topic like a NASA engineer, which was precisely what his first career had been.

He sighed and returned to his recliner, prompting Katherine to smile as she remembered a man who would never have even spoken a word to her the day she first saw him in Cocoa Beach, so very long ago.

She had been a server at Bernard's Surf in Cocoa Beach, working as many shifts as she could. With the Apollo Program in full swing and Cocoa Beach housing many of the new employees at NASA, the restaurant filled nearly every night. One of the benefits of Katherine's job was flirting with all the new young technicians, engineers, and support staff NASA hired.

She did not notice John right away. Unlike the other young men, John sat alone and was absorbed in writing something in a notebook. He mumbled when she came to take his order, and only briefly looked up at Katherine.

It was not until John had come in to eat at Bernard's three nights in a row that Katherine realized he was not anything like the other men, and frankly, she was tired of other men. Who was this timid man, she wondered, who ordered the same meal every night and was oblivious to his surroundings? Katherine loved a good challenge, and as she brought him his check that third night, she whispered to herself, "Just watch, I am going to solve this one!"

Now 50 years later they sat near each other, surrounded by the objects that intimately described their lives. He sat amidst notebooks, sheet music, a violin case, and newspapers. Though cluttered, everything was neatly piled in exact places, satisfying his electrical and mechanical engineer brain. Though the Apollo Program ended decades before, John was still an incessant learner, reader, and loved figuring out how things work.

Katherine on the other hand, was surrounded with unfinished projects chaotically strewn about. Her chair sat with a half-cro-cheted blanket draped over one arm, a few not quite completed letters, and dozens of just started books. Katherine's eyes began to close with drowsiness, her husband's prattling voice about calories and meals serving as white noise to put her to sleep.

Her sleeping these days was much more than normal, a mix of memory and dreaming, but mostly memories.

A knock on the door jolted Katherine back to reality. Sarah, in her crisp blue suit, single, 45, and an attentive niece when her schedule allowed, bustled into the house.

Sarah stopped abruptly in front of Katherine's chair as if she'd run into a wall. "Auntie Kate! Are you feeling okay?" A look of concern appeared on Sarah's face. "Your skin is so yellow! Uncle John, how long has she looked like this?" Alarm wrapped around each word.

John spoke without making eye contact "Yellow? Is it yellow? Katherine is fine, just needs to eat more breakfast and stop napping." John bent down to pick up his violin, preparing to play something, apparently uninterested in the color of Katherine's skin. Sarah had only known her uncle as a violinist, his second professional career, and his violin had become like a third appendage, always connected to him.

Katherine closed her eyes again without speaking, finding it too hard to stay awake. This prompted Sarah to re-address John in a stern tone. "Uncle John, this is serious!" John seemed not to hear as he played the E string, tuning it by ear. She tried again, "Uncle John, please stop for a minute!" John paused and his eyes briefly caught Sarah's before turning downward to the antique violin. He had stopped tuning, which Sarah knew meant her eccentric uncle was indeed listening. "Aunt Kate looks really sick. So sick, that I think we need to call an ambulance." Silence crept into the space. Sarah knew it was best to let her uncle process.

"Let's see, let's see," John began, "she's missed four breakfasts in a row, three lunches, and one dinner this week. That is eight missed out of a potential of 12 meals, which is 67%. Last week she missed 25%. The statistical increase in missed meals does seem relevant. A medical check is likely necessary. I concur."

"Yes, uncle, an ambulance is necessary," Sarah said with reserved anger.

Even though she had been like their own child, Sarah had never gotten used to John's brilliance with numbers, facts, and ways at looking at life. She often wondered why the couple never chose to have children but decided Uncle John must have thought it was not a logical thing to do. Despite occasionally feeling upset with him, she loved him dearly.

Katherine groaned with pain, and Sarah quickly grabbed her cell from her purse and felt heavy with concern as she dialed 911.

The next two days were a blur. Lab tests, scans, and x-rays intermingled with different teams of medical staff. John kept track of each visiting team member, recording the information they shared.

By the afternoon of the second day, a new team walked into the pristine hospital room. Katherine wasn't aware of their entrance and remained asleep as she had been for most of the last few days. While she slept, memories from the past bombarded her. She remembered the pleasure of winning John's interest after weeks of pushing herself into his life when he dined nightly at the restaurant. She always made sure she waited his table, and one night she slid into the booth opposite him and closed his notebook, forcing him to look up at her.

She still saw in her mind his horrified and bewildered expression. She knew her grin was mischievous when she said with confidence, "That's enough of that. I have a few questions for you NASA man." Her mind drifted forward, reliving the first time he played his violin for her in his sparsely furnished apartment.

The passionate music had been in such contrast to his cold and ordered living space, that she had a hard time merging both personas. The music had opened something inside her that night, and she knew she was falling in love. That memory took her to the warm rush of promise she experienced on her wedding day as they stood before the Justice of the Peace, her pregnant sister Karol and brother-in-law serving as witnesses. She wanted to stay in these pleasant memories forever.

Meanwhile, the three-person team swarmed around Katherine's bed. First, the doctor in the group leaned close to Katherine's ear and gently introduced herself, "Katherine, hello!" Katherine's eyes stayed closed but there was a distinct smile on her face as the Doctor continued, "I wanted to introduce myself. I am Dr. Williams. Your primary doctor has asked our team to come by to see how we can help you. If it's alright with you I'm going to sit now and visit with your husband." The team allowed for a response and when there was none, Dr. Williams calmly walked towards John, bringing one of the room chairs close to where John was sitting.

"Are you Mr. Barnes?" Dr. Williams asked, holding out her hand for a greeting.   John, who had been holding one of his many spiral notebooks in his hand, nodded and returned the handshake. "Her urine output today so far is 400ml which is up from 350ml last shift," John informed the new team surrounding him.

Dr. Williams acknowledged this information with feigned interest, while introducing the two advanced practice nurses with her and explaining that she was a palliative care doctor. She clarified that their team's role was to help John process all the information collected over the last two days and help John make important decisions on the direction Katherine's care should head.

At the end of the hour-long discussion, and after the palliative care team had excused themselves, John immediately opened his notebook and wrote down a summary.

"September 21, 4:30pm. Palliative Care Team. Official diagnosis Cholangiocarcinoma (cancer of the bile duct.) Options: 1) Attempt surgery to remove large mass causing blockage and leading to jaundice, liver failure. Risk of surgery is high with 90% chance of complications, 50% chance of death during surgery. Not recommended, not curative. 2) Supportive care for symptoms, which includes transfer to an acute inpatient hospice house. Recommended. Prognosis- days to one week."

As John finished writing, his cell phone rang. He neatly closed his notebook and put down his pencil, in no hurry to answer his phone. Finally, he answered and heard Sarah's voice asking for updates. John was very matter of fact as he conveyed, "She has cholangiocarcinoma, Sarah. This explains her jaundice. The bile duct drains bile from the liver. The tumor is blocking that, so all the bilirubin from the liver cannot drain. It causes the jaundice."

There was a pause. "Oh, Uncle John, I am so sorry to hear this," Sarah lamented. "What is the plan now? Will she begin treatment?"

John went on, unfazed, "No, no treatment. The statistical chance of meaningful recovery is nil. They are going to transfer her to the Hospice House tomorrow morning."

"Hospice? Uncle John, does that mean she doesn't have long to live? Oh, poor Auntie Kate!" Clearly crying on the phone, Sarah tried to wrap her mind around this news. Her own mother, Karol, had died 20 years earlier. Katherine and Karol had been more than sisters, they had been best friends. Aunt Kate had been a constant figure in her childhood and easily slipped into the role of mother when Karol passed. Sarah suddenly felt the pervasive threat of aloneness.

"She has been having pain from the blockage of the duct and they will be able to treat her pain better at the Hospice House," John added, avoiding the question about death. Sarah found it hard to converse with John's factual tone and was overwhelmed with her own emotions. She excused herself from the call, promising to visit that evening.

✱✱

The discharge and transfer to the Hospice House the next morning went smoothly. John entered the large double oak front doors of the house with his violin case in his right hand and several notebooks situated under his left arm.

The ambulance transferring Katherine had preceded John, allowing the hospice staff to be watching for him. Meagan greeted John as one of the social workers of the house. "Welcome, John. The nurses and Doctor are getting Katherine situated in her new room and assessing her. Let me walk you there. As you may know, you are welcome to stay here with her, as each of the rooms has a fold out bed." Meagan continued sharing information as the two walked down a wide corridor with beige walls and earth toned carpet. They passed a large family room with a wall of 8-foot floor to ceiling windows revealing well-manicured gardens.

As Meagan shared the amenities of the Hospice House, John simply walked, slightly hunched over, eyes focused on the floor in front of him. He made no acknowledgement of the information Meagan shared.

They arrived at room 15 just as a thirty-something year old woman with a stethoscope around her neck was stepping out, closing Katherine's door behind her.

"You must be John Barnes," the professionally dressed woman said placing a hand on his right shoulder in greeting. "I'm Dr. Audrey Clark and am going to be Katherine's doctor here. I have just seen her, and the nurses are just finishing up getting her situated. I was hoping we could sit and talk for a few minutes so I can hear a little more about what's been happening these last few days and weeks."

"That would be acceptable." John added, "I have all of her data from the last 2 days in the hospital which I am sure you will want to digest."

"Excellent."

Audrey listened as John provided information from his notebook. Pages full of blood pressures, temperatures, oxygen saturations, pulse rates, and urine outputs.

When the room became quiet, Audrey gently asked John to tell her about Katherine. John furrowed his brow, puzzled; he just looked at her and then the wall.

"For instance, do you have children?"

"No."

"Did Katherine work outside the home?"

"Early on she had many jobs: server, retail, cleaning, secretarial."

"And interests, Mr. Barnes, what are things that interest her?"

John's brows once again knit into one of concentration. After some silence, Audrey tried again, "What did she like to do, besides work?"

Finally, his face relaxed, having found an answer to the question. "Listen to music," he stated. In his mind he saw a middle-aged Katherine, dressed in a black evening gown, sitting on the front row of the Lyric Theater. From his place on stage, despite the bright floodlights, he always sought out her familiar face at the beginning and at the end of each symphony concert. Not once in 13 years had she been absent.

"You seem to have a firm grasp on what is happening to her medically, but do you understand what the end result of all this is?"

"Her overall blood pressures were much higher yesterday at the hospital, which is a good sign, I think."

"John, your wife's body is shutting down," Audrey paused searching John's face for any registration of her words, she pressed on gently, "She only has a few days to live."

John cocked his head just slightly, and then went back to his data about Katherine that he had memorized. Audrey listened patiently and knew inherently not to push anymore.

✳✳✳

The following morning as Audrey made her way to the nurse's station in Pod B she observed John shuffling down the hallway with his violin case in hand. John was a few paces in front of her, and she realized he was wearing the same outfit as the previous afternoon. Green polyester pants, a navy blue knit sweater covering a yellow and blue striped stiff collared shirt. On his head rested a blue and yellow knit stocking cap. As she quickly covered the distance between them, she took in the musty odor of someone who did not bathe frequently.

Audrey was soon parallel to John and immediately slowed

her pace to match his. "Good morning, John. I was just getting ready to go in and see Katherine. Is that a violin case?"

"I play the violin." He stated in his usual to-the-point manner and then, on his own he spoke again. "Yes, I play daily. I used to play with the Kansas City Symphony, first chair." Audrey grinned at this first tiny opening into this man's world.

As they entered the room, the shades were drawn, the room dark except for one piercing lamp situated by an overstuffed chair. Mimicking his chair at home, John had placed piles around in a familiar order. Katherine lay in a discretely disguised hospital bed with two pillows propping up her head. Her eyes were closed, and she had an unnatural yellow ochre skin tone.

John went immediately to his chair, some distance away from his wife's bed, and sat while Audrey addressed Katherine and did an exam of her lungs, heart, and skin.

Katherine never responded outwardly, yet inwardly the assault of past events continued to flash through Katherine's mind like a rolodex of picture cards. Katherine saw their first home and felt pride, experienced the mix of excitement and fear watching the Apollo 7 launch, and she recalled the pleasure of reading to her niece Sarah as a child. Intermixed with the delightful visions would be pangs of grief as she relived each of her five miscarriages. The agony of dashed hopes flooded her being. She watched herself in third person as she cried privately during the middle of the day, so lonely she wanted to scream. She heard the desperation in her voice when she pleaded with John for them to move to Kansas City so she could at least be near her sister Karol. She felt joy radiate out of her center, while pushing the dark memories out, as she recalled the golden years when they first moved to Kansas City. In those years, John would be home practicing violin hours at a time. Sarah was grown and out of the home, and Karol and Katherine spent time together every day.

Subconsciously, she knew where the timeline was taking her, so with what control she had she willed herself to linger in those precious days a little longer.

Audrey finished and came near to John, wanting to discuss what was happening with Katherine. John had opened his notebook with all of his recordings in them, offering his own assessment of how she was doing.

Audrey listened patiently to John's numbers of blood pressures and such before speaking. "You are very detailed, John, and I appreciate that. Now, I wanted to tell you some of the things I am seeing. The main change has been in Katherine's sleeping. You have probably noticed that she seems deeper today. The nurses tell me she has not responded to them. That fact, coupled with her small amount of urine output overnight, and the fever she has today leads me to believe that she is transitioning into the dying process." Audrey paused, allowing the information to sink in.

John looked back at his blood pressure sheet and spoke, "Her blood pressure this morning was 105/70 which is similar to the hospital readings yesterday."

"Yes," Audrey acknowledged, "I would guess you would begin to see those numbers lower in the next day or two. That will help indicate her transition is through." She continued, "I want to make sure you know that despite her deep sleep, she can still hear you. Continue to speak to her, making an effort to say the important things you want to say in this limited time."

John looked down to one of his piles containing violin music; he picked the pile up and began to shift through the paper, completely disengaged in the conversation. Audrey, almost imperceptibly, shook her head, trying not to resent that John was letting these precious moments slip away.

✶✶✶

Soon it was night, though Katherine was no longer aware of time.   Her life review, playing out in her mind, had moved forward to a memory Katherine dreaded: Karol's death.   She watched as she sat with Karol in a hospital room, holding her hand. Karol's face was peaceful but gaunt and pale. It was the last image she had of her sister alive. Her heart ached with grief. She watched the funeral unfold and then felt the loneliness return.   She relived her darkest days, isolated in her home despite John's presence.   A few tears rolled down her slumbering face. Her mind then transported her to her 60th birthday. Sarah sat to her left and John to her right. John fidgeted more than usual during their dessert.   She saw Sarah reach for John's hand and say, 'It's time.' John went to get his violin as Sarah explained, "I told Uncle John that for your 60th birthday he should write you a song." In that moment, John transformed before her eyes.   As he played his first self-composed piece, she felt connected to him in a way she never had before.   More memories of their growing old together surfaced, with the gentle acceptance of what life had become settling upon her.   As her life review ended, a serene peace came over her.

✶✶✶

The next morning Angela, the nurse caring for Katherine,

alerted Audrey that she was actively dying. As Audrey entered the room, she recognized the rapid rhythmic breathing Katherine was experiencing known as agonal breathing. This confirmed in her mind what the numbers revealed. Next, she glanced at John who stood near his chair, once again shuffling papers.

Her heart ached at his distance, even as his wife was clearly dying. Audrey explained the physical signs and again encouraged him to be a part of this process with his wife.

John looked at Katherine briefly. There was a flicker of sorrow across his face, but then he sat in his chair, running his finger down the column of blood pressure readings. Audrey knelt next to John and rested her hand on his arm. Tenderly she said, "I'm going to give you some privacy. John it won't be long now; a few minutes, maybe an hour or two before she passes away."

Before she left the room, Audrey went again to Katherine's bed and took her hand. The skin was both clammy and cool at the same time. John saw Audrey bend to Katherine's ear and speak but could not make out the parting words.

Not 30 minutes passed before Angela found Audrey, noting Katherine was almost gone. Once again in the room, Katherine's face appeared drained of color and her mouth opened but no air rushed in or out. John stood by his chair, his violin tucked, string side out, beneath his right arm, his hand gripping the bow, his gaze down towards the floor. He shifted his weight noticeably back and forth from right to left in a rocking movement. Audrey resisted the urge to force John to come over to the bedside. Instead, she and Angela went to either side of Katherine's bed and took each hand, their eyes watching Katherine's chest for movement. Her chest was motionless. Audrey searched the emptiness of Katherine's lifeless face, wondering about her marriage to John. Did you ever connect with him, she mused, feeling sad that two strangers held her hands, though her husband was just feet away.

Suddenly in the silence, the piercing sound of the violin began. The strings mimicked a human cry, and startled Audrey out of her mournful reverie. The tune was haunting and sorrowful. John's eyes were closed, and his upper body moved with the emotion of the song. His previous timid posture and choppy movements were gone, as his right arm directed the bow across the strings with confidence. Tears began to fall down his cheeks as he played passionately. The sheet music for the song hovered on the arm of the chair, though John clearly had the song memorized. Across the top of the music was the title of the piece: *Irish Lament.*

Audrey and Angela's eyes filled with tears. It was as if each note played was John's own voice, weeping. It was a beautiful moment, not only because the Celtic song of grief captured the emotion in the room, but also because Audrey finally glimpsed John's emotive self. Audrey squeezed Katherine's cold hand with new understanding. It was clear now that what he could not express in word or touch, his music carried for him.

10. FORCED

Maggie

"I've waited my entire life to find my perfect love, and here you are," said the ruggedly handsome man in Maggie's dream. His face looked like Kevin Costner initially, and then morphed into Pierce Brosnan as he spoke, eyes searing fire into Maggie's soul. Maggie blushed and her heart quickened. She opened her mouth to speak, when suddenly a haunting melody of violin music pierced the room. Like a buoy suddenly released from the depths of the ocean, she surfaced into wakefulness.

The weightlessness of her dream world was replaced with the heaviness of her dilapidated state of health. Maggie blinked twice, the hospice room coming into focus. It was late morning, she assumed by the receding shadow lengths of objects on the wall. Her bones ached and her muscles were stiff from being in bed for too long. The skin of her abdomen was taut with fluid, and she felt the sensation of a basketball being inflated past capacity with every breath she took. It was the nausea that bothered her the most, though. The slightest movement sent waves rippling up her stomach, like she was at sea in a storm.

A prickling impression spread from her neck down her back as the sound of violin music continued to pulse from the wall behind her head. The tune grated her nerves and anger boiled. She had been sleeping, dreaming in fact, she thought, and now this! Irritated, her right hand vigorously patted the area on her bed, looking for the plastic box. Finding the call light, she pressed the small raised button continuously until the sound of the intercom on her bed turned on.

"Can I help you?" a nondescript female voice said.

"Yes!" Maggie nearly screamed. "Get someone to stop that violin music; I was trying to sleep!" She thought she heard someone say okay, but she kept talking anyway. "I thought this place was supposed to be peaceful and quiet. Aren't there rules about instruments? Maybe someone should have asked me if it was okay to play."

Maggie was still talking to no one in particular when her door opened and Angela, the nurse, walked in. Angela was in her 20's and had an enthusiastic kindness that irritated Maggie.

"What can I do for you, Maggie?" Angela said, with a slight catch in her voice. Maggie noticed some red blotches around Angela's eyes. The thought that Angela had been crying brought Maggie some pleasure.

"That God forsaken music next door, someone needs to stop it!" Maggie paused, suddenly realizing the music had stopped. "Well, good, I'm glad someone took care of that."

Angela wanted to explain to Maggie that a woman had just

died next door. Confidentiality, however, wouldn't allow that, so Angela just nodded and asked if there was anything else she could do.

"Could you tell my Doctor I have some things I want to discuss?"

Angela nodded, her emotions were still connected to the patient next door, and she just wanted to leave the room. Maggie had been at the Hospice House less than 24 hours and already she was earning the reputation of being difficult. Angela knew the metastatic ovarian cancer Maggie had was painful and terrifying, but Maggie wasn't letting anyone help her. All she seemed to do was complain.

As Angela left Maggie's room, she saw Dr. Audrey Clark a few paces down the hall. "Dr. Clark," Angela called, happy to pass Maggie's troubles off to someone else. Audrey turned; she too had puffy eyes from the experience they had shared earlier with the patient who had died.

"Maggie wants to 'discuss' something with you." Angela didn't hide her sarcasm.

Audrey hadn't had many interactions yet with Maggie and naïvely agreed to tackle the challenge immediately. She reached for a folded paper in her front pants pocket. The paper was her second brain, and contained a print out of each patient, room number and diagnosis. Audrey spent each morning making further notes in the margins to remind her of issues and key information.

Audrey met Maggie late the afternoon before, during her admission, but in her eagerness to finish the day and get home, she had not spent a lot of time in conversation. Her chicken scratch notes refreshed her mind; single, 53, found tumor 3 months ago, refused treatment, pain and nausea.

Entering the room, Audrey scrutinized her patient. Maggie sat up in bed with her eyes closed. She had greasy shoulder length brown hair, pulled into a low pony tail. Thick out-of-date glasses framed her pale skin and she had more wrinkles than expected for her age. The most prominent crevasses accentuating a resting frown. She was overweight even without the swollen abdomen filled with fluid and tumor.

Maggie's eyes opened, sensing Audrey's presence, and immediately narrowed as she did her own dissecting. "You are younger than I remember yesterday, but then again, you seemed in a hurry to leave. I didn't have much time to notice."

"I apologize for that. It was late in the day, and I thought you'd be more refreshed today to spend some time together." Audrey pulled the chair next to the bed out and at an angle, so she could sit almost face to face with Maggie. "Before we get to the items you wanted to discuss, I was interested to know more of your history. For example, how did you find the ovarian cancer?"

At this Maggie dramatically rolled her eyes, which was followed by a pained expression. "Do you know Dr. Kane?"

Audrey shook her head negatively.

"What a joke of a doctor. I had been seeing him for months, complaining of stomach pain. I kept telling him something was wrong, but he didn't listen. Just gave me different medicines to take, told me to lose weight, things like that." She checked to make sure Audrey was being attentive before continuing. "I shouldn't have been surprised; no one ever takes me seriously."

Audrey ignored the direct challenge and bait for sympathy and instead asked, "But how did you finally find the tumor?"

"He ordered a scan finally, and there it was, my belly full of cancer, just as I had suspected." Her tone still irritated she added, "Then he wanted to treat me! As if I'd let that screw-up try to fix this!"

Audrey looked puzzled. "What about seeing someone else for treatment?"

"What would be the point? Doctors are all the same. Plus, I hate medicine, it always makes me worse."

"Did any of your friends or family think differently?"

Maggie looked as if she were going to laugh, her eyes opened in amusement. "What friends? What family?" Maggie shook her head slightly, "My parents adopted me when they were nearing 40. They both died years ago. As for friends, one by one they've betrayed me and left."

"Wow, I'm sorry." Audrey genuinely felt bad for this woman. Not wanting to linger on this, she changed topics, "Let's move on to today. How are you feeling symptom-wise?"

Audrey noticed a shift in Maggie's appearance with the question, almost as if Maggie was metamorphosing. Her shoulders hunched inward, her eyes squinted, and a grimace formed. Her voice became less haughty and feebler, "Miserable."

"Oh? What specifically is causing you to be miserable?"

"I've been vomiting. I hurt. I am so tired that I can hardly speak." With this, Maggie's voice faded into a whisper and her hand came up to rest on her neck.

"You're in luck, because we have things that can help with your misery." Audrey purposefully looked confident as she spoke, fully aware she was going to try and sell Maggie the idea that she could be helped. "You have a medicine called Haldol to take for your vomiting. You can take it every two hours if you need. You also have Morphine for your pain."

Maggie was dismissive, "I've tried all of those things, and they don't work."

"You've had Haldol before? I'm surprised. It's not one most

doctors use."

"Maybe not that one, but I'm sure it won't work. Nothing ever does."

Audrey's jaw clenched while maintaining a pleasant aura, "I'll tell you what. Let's give it a try today. You may be correct, it might not work. However, it also might really help. You say you are miserable, and I'd like to alleviate some of that." Audrey paused and added, "Please let me try."

Maggie heard the slight desperation in Audrey's voice and the image of Audrey kneeling on the ground and pleading for Maggie to try, popped into her brain, causing a slight smile to emerge.

"Fine. I'll try, but you'll see, it won't help."

Feeling slightly victorious, Audrey rose and bid Maggie a good day, promising to check-in the next morning. When she reached the door to leave, she heard Maggie lament, "Good day, like that's even possible!"

The moment the door closed, Maggie was aware of her alone-ness. It was the sensation she dreaded most. At least here she could ring a button, and someone would appear. When she had been at home, she'd sometimes call five different people, until someone finally agreed to come take her to the store or take her to an appointment. She couldn't understand why people were so busy and unwilling to help. Life had been unfair to her in that respect.

Maggie thought of her last boyfriend, Chuck. They had met at the laundromat 2 years ago. Chuck loved going to the movies as much as Maggie, and they had formed an easy friendship around that. After a few weeks, they were spending everyday together. Then, just like every other person, he faltered. Chuck had been invited on a fishing trip with his cousin. Maggie had spent the weekend alone and depressed, calling Chuck every few hours. She was worried that he would meet someone new or enjoy his cousin more than her.

When he got back, she could hardly make it out of bed from her depressed state. He passed the test though and came to her apartment and nursed her back to life by reading to her, fixing her food, and encouraging her to get out of bed.

This became the pattern, a few good weeks, then he'd have to be gone, she'd get ill, and he'd make things better. Each time, he seemed to resent his role more and more, and Maggie grew more paranoid of losing him. As he drifted away, she became more desperate. A few times, Maggie was so distraught she ingested a handful of Tylenol pills, or at least threatened to if he didn't come to see her.

As Maggie thought back to the final time she and Chuck spoke, she grew angry. He had refused to come over one evening. She had called a dozen times and he wouldn't answer. She took more pills than she should have and kept calling. Finally, he picked up.

"You better get over here," she said, "I've taken a bottle of pills and I think this is the end."

"I told you, Maggie, I will not come over, and I want to be done with this relationship." His voice was stern. He had tried to break up with her before, but she didn't believe he was serious.

"So, you're just going to let me die?" she had screamed. "I guess you'll have to live with yourself when you find out I'm gone."

"Maggie, if you have really taken a bottle of pills, then I'm calling an ambulance. But I'm not coming over."

She had been livid. The nerve of him! So uncaring, that he was willing to let her die. All she had wanted was to have him come over. She hung up, knowing that she wouldn't speak to him again. He was just like every other person in her life; he had let her down and left her alone.

The memory faded and Maggie's stomach cramped as a wave of nausea washed over her. She reached for the call light; she needed someone in her room immediately.

✷✷✷

It was still dark when Angela entered the Hospice House the following morning. This was day four of a five day stretch and she was in a slump. It was 6:40 A.M., and she hadn't left work until 9 P.M. the night before, trying to get her charting caught up. She stopped in the staff kitchen area to put her lunch of yogurt, a cheese stick, and candy bar into the refrigerator. The chance she'd actually get to sit and eat was slim. After tomorrow, she reminded herself, she'd be off work for an entire week.

On her way to Pod B, she saw her good friend Caron was already sitting down ready to get checkout from the two night nurses.

"It's about time you showed up," Caron greeted, with a twinkle in her eye. Angela was just about to respond when she saw a pink plastic princess scepter sitting on the nurse's desk at her spot.

"What is this?" she asked, seeing now that all three nurses were grinning.

Caron responded, "You had such a rough day yesterday with room 16, I thought you needed this. Since Maggie seems to think she's the queen, I wanted to empower you to have your own queen gear. Each time she calls for you, you need to wave your wand to get into the kingdom mind frame."

They all laughed as Angela picked up the toy and waved it regally and mimicked Maggie. "Angela, there is a wrinkle in my sheet, please straighten it. Angela, I need 15 ice cubes in my water, 13 just will not do."

Angela put her scepter down, still chuckling and asked Cindy, the 50-year-old night nurse, how Maggie had been.

"Not as bad as you had it. I was in there probably seven times, usually because of pain or nausea. But of course she took nothing."

"Sounds like I'm going to have another great day," Angela said sarcastically, picking up the pink princess gear and giving the other nurses a regal christening. They all burst into raucous laughter just as Audrey entered the hallway from the parking lot, passing the nurses' station.

The laughter was infectious, and Audrey found herself grinning and drawn to the commotion as an outsider longing to be a part of the joke.

"What is so funny?" Audrey asked eagerly, coming closer.

Angela explained the scepter and began to mimic Maggie. However, noting Audrey's brow wrinkling and a frown forming, the act fizzled rapidly. Angela tried to shrink into herself and said sheepishly, "I guess, maybe not so appropriate?"

Audrey abhorred reprimanding and tried to be light hearted when she said, "Look, I get it, she's tough to care for. Let's just not be disrespectful." The group of nurses nodded kindly, but as Audrey turned to head to her desk, she could imagine them rolling their eyes.

✳✳✳

Angela had already been in Maggie's room four times when Audrey stepped out of room 17 and came down for an update.

Angela addressed Audrey, "You were in Frank's room for a while. Any luck with convincing him to take medication? I can't believe I have two patients refusing meds."

"I think I might have, actually. It was a fascinating visit. He's doing such hard work. I doubt I'll be so lucky with Maggie. How is she today?" As Audrey spoke the delight embedded on her face from being with Frank morphed into trepidation as she realized the impending challenge that Maggie's visit was next.

"She's pretty bad, Dr. Clark. I can tell she is really hurting, but she still hasn't had any medication."

Audrey felt a slight squeeze in her chest. She was not looking forward to this.

"Tell me, Angela, is she eating anything? Having bowel movements?"

"Nothing besides water and ice, she says she's too sick for food. As for BM's, nothing while here and she said it had been at least a week before she was admitted since her last one."

Audrey nodded, making notes on her paper and glancing at the Nurses' log of vitals and notes.

"It's so frustrating." Angela continued, "I even tried sneaking some morphine in her orange juice this morning, hoping it would help."

Audrey's head snapped up, eyes wide. "You tried to trick her into taking something?"

"Of course! She is clearly suffering and in pain. I just wanted to help her." Angela wasn't sure if she was in trouble, Audrey didn't look mad, but something was amiss. She couldn't imagine she'd done anything wrong, though.

Audrey put down her pen and struggled to find the right

words. "Angela, you are a good nurse." At this she smiled with compassion and warmth. "But you just can't trick people. Maggie has so little control of things; you'll end up taking away the last of her autonomy."

Angela was honestly struggling with this. "How can giving someone what they need be a bad thing?"

Audrey brought her pen to the side her mouth and began rattling it on her teeth as she concentrated. The corners of her mouth turned upward as a thought came to her. "Okay then, I'm going to order you to a strict regimen of salad greens." Angela pouted dramatically, her co-workers all knew she had a quirky aversion to salads.

"Fine, you win." Angela said in mock anger, and then added a zinger as she got up to leave, "I guess that's why they pay you the big bucks." Audrey's mouth opened in pretend disgust as Angela walked away.

Mentally Audrey changed gears and prepped herself for getting frustrated and walked to Maggie's room. Very intentionally, she made her voice as cheery as possible and greeted Maggie with a smile.

"Morning, Maggie." Audrey waited for Maggie to open her eyes, "How are you feeling today?"

"Is it still morning? What time do you even get to work?"

Audrey would not let herself be goaded, "I certainly wish you were my only patient, but I do have many people to see each day." Audrey came and sat next to Maggie and waited for her to answer the original question.

"I'm sure Angela told you. I'm horrible today, just awful."

"Oh?" Audrey said, feigning a bit of surprise, "I was hoping the medicines would be helping, tell me did they bring even a little relief?" Audrey knew they were in a dance, a charade in which each party knew the role to play.

"I haven't taken anything, because it will make me feel worse."

"That's too bad. You really are in a tough spot then."

Maggie did not like this response. She had hoped the doctor would have had a more sympathetic reply. Feeling irritated Maggie asked, "What are you going to do then? How are you going to help me?"

Audrey shrugged her shoulders in an exaggerated way. Earlier in her career Audrey would not have responded like this. She used to plead with and cajole patients. The problem was if a patient was determined not to be helped, they wouldn't acknowledge the medicine's benefit. She'd wasted a lot of effort convincing people to try things they didn't believe in. Even when the evidence pointed to the medication having an effect, often those patients would adamantly deny their value.

It was time to be direct with Maggie.

"The reality is you most likely have a bowel obstruction. The tumor is large enough that food can't pass through. This is causing the pain and nausea you are experiencing. It is not something easily fixed." Audrey could see anger written on Maggie's face, but she continued, "There are two paths for you." Audrey stretched out her right hand, "One is to let us manage the symptoms from the obstruction. I would prescribe steroids, nausea and pain medicines that have helped countless people I've taken care of with this exact problem. "

Maggie interrupted, "That's not a path! I can't take medicines, they make things worse."

Audrey pushed away the annoyance she felt and continued, "The second option is to transfer to a hospital. You would revoke hospice and seek treatment. They would put a tube down your nose to decompress the fluid and air trapped. A surgeon would look to see if an operation might help to remove the tumor. They would work aggressively to fix the obstruction. There's a good chance, though, you wouldn't leave the hospital."

Maggie's eyes widened in horror as she spoke, "A tube down my nose? The harassment of nurses and doctors coming to poke and prod me day and night? The IV's and incessant beeping keeping me from rest? How is that an option?"

Audrey now had both hands out, palms up, indicating the two paths. "Of course, you can choose neither, and you will be as you are now; miserable."

Maggie's face was red, and Audrey wondered if steam might be about to flow out of her ears. She braced herself for the eruption.

"And you call yourself a doctor; A 'healer.'" Maggie exploded with disdain. "They say hospice is about comfort and about dignity, but this is ridiculous. I have gotten worse in the time I've been here. You have nothing to offer me and in your own words, you say I am going to remain miserable." Maggie paused, ignoring the cramping pain in her abdomen. "I may have to transfer just to get away from your incompetence," she threatened.

Audrey tried deflecting the insults, but the arrows still left a mark before falling away. "I'm sorry you feel that way. If you do decide to transfer, I'll be sure to make the arrangements promptly." Audrey rose, ready to flee the vehemence.

"That's all you have to say? I'm sorry? Well you will be sorry, I'm going to make sure and tell everyone at the hospital what a scam this place is." Maggie was leaning forward, and a few drops of spit flew from her mouth as she spoke.

"I guess I'll make the phone call now." Audrey said calmly and turned to exit.

In panic mode Maggie escalated, "You've wanted me out of

here since I arrived, haven't you? I have never met a more un-loving doctor. You're actually cruel! I bet you work in hospice because the only people who will tolerate you are half dead!"

Audrey did not even look back at Maggie, but left the room, shut the door, and walked briskly into the public bathroom directly across the hall. Thankfully, no one was in the one-person restroom. She locked the door and stood frozen. Her heart raced, and she felt tears form in her eyes, and she disliked the weakness of caring what Maggie thought of her. "Do not cry," she spoke softly to herself, "She is a sad, lonely woman who is terri-fied of dying. She is just looking for people to blame."

Audrey walked a pace to the mirror and looked for signs of being rattled. She had spoken her tears back inside and didn't see evidence of the near emotional collapse. She adjusted her stethoscope around her neck and ran her thumb across her name badge. She nodded to her reflected self in the mirror and left to make arrangements for Maggie's departure.

Back in the room Maggie tried to calm her breathing. The outburst had caused intense pain, like a cat wearing nails as shoes was walking on top of her belly. "These people," she said out loud in a clenched voice from the pain, "forcing me out."

Tears began to cascade down Maggie's face. It was unfair. Why did people always make her do things she didn't want to do? She thought of the day her parents had forced her to leave home. She was 16, and had been spending time with Ricky, an 18-year-old trouble maker that her parents did not like. Ricky was sometimes hard on her, telling her she was stupid or fat, but those were true things, and she loved him, and he seemed to need her. Ricky wanted her to drop out of school and move in with him, but she was just scared enough of his temper that she had said no.

Then her parents gave her an ultimatum. They said, "You either start making curfew, and quit missing school, or you cannot live under this roof." She was upset that they were trying to interfere with her life. It wasn't her fault that Ricky kept her out past curfew, or that he would be waiting for her at school in the morning and need her to spend time with him, instead of being in school. She didn't really have a choice. Her parents kicked her right into hell, and she never forgave them for that.

That same bitterness tinged with fear coated her throat now as it had 45 years ago, but what choice did she have?

✳✳✳

The news that Maggie was leaving was an unexpected gift to the staff. In the 48 hours she had been at the Hospice House, Maggie had managed to provoke three to lose their tempers and two to leave her room in tears, this not counting the private tears that people like Audrey had shed.

Audrey was sitting at the nurses' station writing orders on a new patient in room 15, when Angela returned from escorting the ambulance crew out the back with Maggie in tow. She slumped down on her chair and put the tips of her fingers to her temple.

Audrey looked up, noticing Angela seemed strained. "You feel it too?" Audrey picked up the plastic scepter and turned it over and over in her hand examining it.

Angela put her hands down and noticing Audrey's focus, shrugged her shoulders and replied, "If you mean torn and conflicted, then yes."

Audrey replayed Maggie's verbal attacks in her mind. She welcomed the relief that came from knowing she wouldn't have to endure anymore of Maggie's darts. When she thought about the hospital environment Maggie was heading into, the system of actions and outcomes, she felt genuinely worried. Experience told her that Maggie still potentially had several grueling weeks to live, and she could surmise those days and weeks would be filled with suffering. The longing to intervene, to fix the unfixable, was sheer torment.

Audrey guessed by the way Angela's eyes were moist and threatening to run over, she was processing similar feelings. Audrey's gaze locked with Angela and she placed the pink plastic scepter into the nurse's hand. "You should keep this out here at the nurses' station." Audrey's own eyes misted, "I don't want to forget Maggie too quickly."

ii. TIES

Albert

The sound of tapping was faint and barely registered in Albert's mind. Where was he, anyway? His breathing was heavy and hard, and he became aware, as he gained consciousness that he was unable to move. His eyes gradually opened, and he registered his dirty linoleum floor. Crumbs, hair, and paper bits seemed like enormous creatures at this view.

The tapping grew to pounding and he thought maybe his name was being called. He was too exhausted to try to move or speak. He wondered if he was dying. There was a heaviness settling on him that tried to draw him back into the deep unawareness that he'd been in before the tapping started.

"Al!" A worried male voice shouted, as his front door opened. He recognized his neighbor's drawl and felt a firm hand on his shoulder, shaking him. He was able to grunt out an unintelligible sound. His neighbor cursed and seemed to be talking to himself, "Where's the damn phone?"

Albert heard rummaging and more curse words and finally a frantic call for an ambulance. He felt himself drifting back to nowhere, feeling comforted now that he knew he was not alone.

✶✶✶

Albert wasn't sure why people hated hospitals so much. He was propped up on two pillows in an ICU bed, crisp clean sheets tucked and tight fitting, and a warm breakfast of crispy bacon and scrambled eggs were placed on his bedside table. The plastic little straw-like tubes in his nose ushering in a fast flow of oxygen seemed like a miracle to him, making his breathing much easier. He hadn't felt this well in over a year. In his small two roomed apartment, he was only able to take three steps before he would hunch forward and put his hands on his knees. He would huff and strain to get air back into his lungs. Five minutes would pass, and his breathing would ease enough to take three more steps and start the process over again.

In fact, with how much better he felt, Albert was having a very hard time reconciling the news his doctor had told him that morning. Dr. Asher, a cardiologist, had explained that Albert's heart was barely functioning. He had used a number; 10%. Was that how little heart he had left, he wondered? He couldn't quite understand it all, but he didn't miss the grim tone of Dr. Asher's words. Dr. Asher had been very clear on one thing; Albert had only a few weeks left to live. Had he been told that news a month ago, when he had woken one night to the sensation that a wall had collapsed on his chest and buried him alive, he might have believed it. Indeed, that night he thought he was dying. But, today, today he felt great.

His contemplation was interrupted by the sound of the ICU glass door sliding open and a young woman with short wavy hair, wearing a white coat, stepping in.

"Hello. You must be Albert Stone?" The woman stepped forward with a wide grin, "I'm Dr. Audrey Clark from the palliative care consult team."

Albert matched the smile, "You're my doctor? How'd I luck out getting a pretty one?" He flirted.

Audrey sidestepped the comment, "I'm actually here at the request of Dr. Asher. He thought with all that's happened over the last few days, that it would be good to sit down and talk." As Audrey spoke, she searched and examined Albert visually, sizing up what she saw with what she had read in the medical chart.

Albert's hollow cheeks and drooping skin on his arms matched the sixty-pound weight loss over the last year. His barrel chest that heaved with each breath fit the lung disease that came from fifty years of smoking. She decided he definitely did not look his stated age of 65, but instead looked at least a decade older.

"Well shoot, let's talk then." Albert patted the side of his bed.

"Actually, I was thinking we should have more of a family meeting. There's a lot to go through."

A cloud descended on Albert's features and he turned his gaze to the wall in front of him.

"Who can I contact for a family meeting?" Audrey tried to be sensitive in asking.

There was a pause of silence and Audrey gently tried again, "Anyone?"

"No one."

"I thought I read that you have three grown children?"

Albert let out a snort, "We don't talk anymore. I haven't seen them in years."

Audrey was about to honor this, and move on with the hard conversation about his disease and what was coming, when a kernel of a thought that she should push him, popped to her mind.

Albert was still drilling a hole into the wall with his forward stare. Audrey placed her hand on the top of his, feeling the slightest flinch, "Are you sure? What's happening now is a really big deal. It might be worth trying.... giving them a chance to respond."

A tear slid from Albert's eye and his gaze lowered. He took a deep breath and with resignation said, "I guess you can try my daughter. She lives on the East coast and who knows if she's even at the same number." He hesitated and added, "Don't expect much."

Audrey squeezed Albert's hand before she turned to go, "Thank you," she whispered.

Back in the small consult room on the 5th floor, Audrey sat in solitude to eat the salad she'd grabbed from the hospital cafeteria. This was the last week of her month doing hospital consults. She and her partners took turns four times a year covering the service. The work load was completely different, upstream, as they called it. Many of the patients she was asked to see were at the beginning of the end and had intense reactions to the new awareness of their own mortality.

Families also tended to act in more extremes in the acute setting of the hospital. She pondered how Albert's daughter would react to her phone call. This had to be the hardest part of her job, she decided, cold calling people with bad news. She swallowed the last of her salad and grabbed the office phone.

A woman picked up after the fourth ring, and Audrey heard childrens' voices in the background. The voice sounded out of breath.

"Hello, I'm trying to reach Tanya Goodall."

"That's me." Audrey heard the immediate hesitation due to the unknown nature of the call.

"This is Dr. Audrey Clark calling from the University of Kansas Hospital about your father, Albert Stone."

The intake of air reverberated in Audrey's ear, "Oh no!" Tanya's voice was panicked.

Audrey rushed to continue, "He came into the hospital three days ago in pretty bad shape, but they've got him stabilized now."

"Thank God he's not dead," the relief was palpable in Tanya's voice, "but what's wrong? What happened?"

"Your father probably had a heart attack on top of chronic heart failure, all of this is also affecting his lungs and kidneys. I'm not sure how long he's been failing at home, he wouldn't see a doctor."

"Figures, that stubborn SOB," Tanya interjected.

"Things have passed the point of no return, I'm sorry to say. Medically there isn't anything to be done to fix years of damage."

"It's the alcohol isn't it?" Tanya had a hint of resentment now.

"Actually, I'm not sure about that. He hasn't been drinking for years, from what I understand."

"Oh, so now he decides to quit! I guess we weren't reason enough!" Anger spilled over and Audrey tried to redirect.

"Tanya, your father gave me permission to call you. He probably only has a few weeks to live. I was hoping to include you in the conversation about what to do from here on out."

While Tanya paused to think, Audrey was able to pick out an infant's whimpering layered on top of the sound of a children's television program.

"Why now?" Tanya said to herself with frustration and then addressed Audrey, "Okay. Yes, I need to do this. I'm going to try to get a flight out tomorrow. Can our meeting wait until I get there?"

Audrey was surprised, expecting just a phone call meeting together. "Of course it can wait. I'm so glad you are coming. It's going to mean so much to your father."

Tanya was shaking when she hung up the phone. She absent-mindedly raked her fingers thru her hair, pulling it back into a ponytail. She stood in a stupor, holding her hair back staring at her living room. Her three-year-old was glued to the T.V., her 8-month-old whimpered in his swing. Tanya's mind, though, didn't register her surroundings, but instead she was back in a memory from her childhood home.

She wasn't sure if it was the screaming or thud of a chair being knocked over that had awoken her. At 15 she usually didn't leave her room in her night shirt, but she ran to the commotion without thinking. Her younger brother Grant had come from his room too, and they both huddled together peering at the scene before them.

Their father loomed like a vulture, taunting and spewing drunken wrath at their mother, who cowered, her tear-streaked face turned into her shoulder as if the words were striking her cheek. Positioned in between, like a basketball player guarding his opponent, their 17-year-old brother Teddy stood in a wide stance, with arms open and waving defensively at their dad while protecting their mother.

"Get out of the way, you good for nothing bastard! Quit protecting that whore!" The words slurred from their father's mouth, his movements jerky and uncoordinated. Tanya let out a scream, instinctively her arm raised to protect Grant. Teddy heard the scream and turned his attention to the sound, noticing his younger siblings for the first time. Tanya saw his eyes were full of fear and anger.

"Go!" Teddy commanded Tanya and Grant frantically. In that moment of distracted focus, their father capitalized on the situation and let lose a left hook punch to Teddy's temple. Teddy stumbled and fell to his hands and knees as Grant and Tanya let out ear splitting shrieks. Blood dripped from Teddy's nose but there was fire in his eyes. He rose and bolted over to their father, shoving him to the wall and pinning him with his forearm.

Teddy's voice dripped with contempt as he spit the words out, "You are leaving this house now. You will never speak to us or see us again."

That was 20 years ago. Despite his absence, she had always known he was still around from the occasional birthday card that would randomly show up or the Kansas number on her caller I.D. that never left a message. The idea of his impending death seasoned her anger and pain with something new. Was it sadness, or pity, or regret that had been broken lose by the phone call? She guessed she would find out soon.

Tanya felt a tug on her shorts and snapped back to the present.

"Mommy, I'm hungry." Her son's bright blue eyes pleaded with her and she mumbled an agreement, walking to the kitchen to get crackers.

A jumble of thoughts bombarded her simultaneously, paralyzing her to any action. She needed to get a flight, pack, and call her husband. Her father was dying. Should she call her brothers? How long would she be gone?

"Mommy!" Her son cried out with exasperation. Tanya was in a fog, standing lifeless in front of the cupboard, but his whining voice cleared the stupor quickly.

"The kids!" She stated to herself, suddenly realizing this was the biggest challenge to her plans. She grabbed a sleeve of Ritz crackers and handed the entire package to her son, whose eye widened at the treat.

Just then the cell phone she clutched tightly in her left hand rang, causing her heart to skip a beat. Tanya saw her sister-in-law's name come across the screen and she smiled. It was payback time for all the occasions Tanya had watched her nieces and nephews.

✷✷✷

Early the next morning, Audrey headed to her 5th floor office to take stock of the day, before the new consults started coming in. The unknowns of whether she'd have five patients to see or fifteen countered her bent towards control, and she was looking forward to getting back to the enclosed environment of the Hospice House. Looking at her patient list on the computer, she decided to stop by the ICU and see Albert first. Dr. Asher had run into her yesterday and wasn't happy for the delay on plans. She had promised that all would be known by the end of this day.

The cardiac ICU was on the 4th floor, so Audrey took the stairs. She could see through the glass doors of Albert's room that a woman near Audrey's age was hovering over Albert. The woman had long brown hair pulled loosely into a ponytail at her neck. She wore a black tattered Led Zeppelin T-shirt and jeans. As Audrey entered the room, she took note of the tears and smiles on both of their faces.

"Sorry to interrupt," Audrey greeted, "Albert, you look quite well this morning."

Tanya, whose hand was interlocked with her father's, looked up, slightly embarrassed by her tears.

"Dr. Clark, this is my daughter, Tanya." Pride oozed from Albert's pores and Audrey clearly detected a new peacefulness there.

"So, you're the one I spoke to on the phone," Tanya asked, "I am so grateful you called." She looked back at her father as fresh tears spilled. "We haven't spoken in 20 years and have so much to say to each other."

They spent the next 30 minutes talking through the medical facts and Audrey guided them through Albert's priorities and hopes, which led them to their discharge plan. Tanya decided she would stay in Kansas to help, and Albert would go home with hospice care in the home setting.

Audrey stood to leave, happy with the plan.

Tanya had a gnawing thought diving in and out of her brain, and finally decided to ask it. "Dad, I was wondering if you'd let me call Teddy?"

As if an electricity line had been cut, the mood chilled instantly. Albert bristled and grunted out a "no". Tanya recoiled but didn't press further. Some of the joy Audrey had been pumped full of during the visit escaped into the air. At least, she thought, he's reconciled with his daughter.

✶✶✶

It was 4:45 P.M. and Audrey sat in her office counting down the minutes. She knew if she tried to sneak away early the hospital gods would torture her with a late consult that she'd be forced to deal with. As soon as she'd had this thought her pager went off and she exclaimed out loud, "You have got to be kidding me!"

She glanced down at the black square device and saw the number to the ICU. Answering the page, Audrey couldn't help but feel like a contestant on a twisted form of the game "What's behind door number three?" You never knew what was on the other end of the phone. It could be a simple question she would answer easily, or an emergency that sucked her into hours more of work.

"Dr. Clark, this is Julie in the ICU," the voice was somewhat frazzled and belonged to one of the younger nurses in the unit. "There's a bit of a disturbance going on down here with Mr. Stone and his daughter. I called Dr. Asher, but he said you would be the one who could handle this."

Audrey only allowed her eyes a half eye-roll and told Julie she'd be down to see what she could do.

Near Albert's room, Audrey saw Tanya pacing. Her fists were balled up to her side and she was staring at the ground as she marched. Julie, the ICU nurse, stood uncomfortably nearby, a look of loss tinged with nervousness on her face. Audrey dove right in.

"Tanya," She tried intertwining smooth and calm into her tone, "Hey, tell me what's going on?"

Tanya looked up and the softness of Audrey's voice was enough to tip the battle that raged inside her between anger and sadness, over to tears. For a moment, before the floodgates opened, Audrey saw a glimpse of a frightened child.

"I don't know what I was thinking, coming here," She hid her face in her hands as she continued, "He's the same ugly person who left us 20 years ago."

Audrey very slowly put her hand on Tanya's shoulder and gave it a squeeze and then withdrew it but said nothing.

"Seeing him like this…," She struggled for words, "…weak and… and small. I felt so bad for him, so guilty for never reaching out." Tanya whimpered and her hands dropped and clasped each other at her chest, as if she was attempting to bottle up something.

"What actually happened in there?" Audrey gestured with her head towards the ICU room.

Disgust enveloped Tanya's expression and anger returned, "I was helping him get something to drink. I thought he had the cup, he thought I did, and the next thing you know it spilled on him." Tanya's eye's darkened, "He reminded me then of my utter worthlessness." Tanya shivered and then she looked up at Audrey, transforming her anger to sheepishness. "I kind of lost it and maybe threw the cup still full of ice and water across the room."

Audrey's vision snapped over to Julie to confirm the story and noted Julie's wide eyes and slight nodding of her head. Audrey turned back to Tanya, who was awaiting a response. Wrinkling up her nose, Audrey muttered the only thing that came to mind, "Yikes!"

Feeling it was her cue to speak into the situation, Audrey lifted her hands as if she were throwing out grain, knowing her words might or might not take root.

"Look, I don't know all that has come between you and your dad, and all the baggage there. One thing I do know, these next few weeks are going to be *really* hard. There will be more of these moments, I'm sure of it." Tanya choked out a burst of laughter, and Audrey continued, "Hopefully, there will be some good moments, too." Audrey crossed her arms in front of her, trying to ascertain if any of this was making a dent. She wrapped up saying, "I hate to say it, but the amount of work that he's going to be able to do on himself, on your relationship, on all of it, is pretty slim. It's really up to you, on how much you can handle."

Tanya nodded and then sighed, a deep and hearty sigh. "I think I'm going to go grab something to eat. I'm not ready to go back in there yet."

Audrey acknowledged this and watched Tanya escape out the double doors of the ICU, the click of the secure and heavy doors reverberating back to Audrey and Julie.

✶✶✶

Tanya stepped out on her father's front stoop, a three foot square block of cement, and dug in her pocket for the cheap lighter she'd picked up at the store two days after taking Albert back home. Tanya had quit smoking when she was pregnant with her first and hated that in the strain of taking care of her father, she'd started again. She lit a cigarette, angrily inhaling the nicotine.

Albert's home consisted of one bedroom, which Albert had graciously lent to Tanya, and a room that functioned as kitchen and living room. The hospital bed placed in the middle of that space, left little space for anything but a television. The constant nearness of her father, his requests and pickiness, were getting to be too much.

She took another draw, the familiar feeling of guilt gnawing at her insides. She was losing her temper too many times a day.

Just then Tanya heard her name being called. She looked up to see her father's neighbor, Jim, signaling her. She sighed, frustrated with the interruption, but smiled at this kind man who had checked in daily to see how Albert was doing.

His drawl was thick and deep, matching his large frame, "Mornin' Surga'. How's your daddy doing today?" Jim had come across the street, not waiting for an invitation.

Tanya cringed at the word, daddy, and exhaled, her nose instinctually wrinkling. Jim misread the expression and added, "I sure am sorry that he's not doing no better." Tanya didn't feel the need to correct Jim and tried to enjoy the last of her cigarette without talking.

Jim easily filled the silence. "Me and your Daddy's been neighbors for a mighty long time, you know?" Tanya nodded her head acknowledging the statement. "I can tell you two is havin' a heck of a time gettin' along."

Tanya rolled her eyes, "What makes you think that?"

Jim missed the sarcasm, "I see how your face looks when you step out here to smoke." Jim paused, "...and I know how Al can be. He's a bit rough at times."

A bitter laugh escaped before Tanya could catch it.

Jim was undeterred, "You ever spend any time tryin' to figure out where that roughness come from?"

Immediate anger exploded within Tanya and she spit out her words, "Don't you go trying to get me to excuse..."

"Listen, no listen," Jim interrupted, "I'm not excusin' nothin'. He told me about some of the awful things he did, things that he hated about himself. But sugar, you can't imagine the awful things that were done to him, neither. The bottle became the only thing that could mellow those demons, it took away the hurt."

"What, like he was bullied or something, so he figured it was okay to bully his family?"

Jim struggled with knowing if he should share more. He hesitated, "It's hard for me to tell it, but, darlin', an older man that was a neighbor of your daddy's when he was little, well, he abused your daddy for years." Jim's voice became gruff as he held back emotion, "and fact is, even when your daddy tried to get his folks to help him, they acted like he was lyin' and kept sendin' him to spend time with that snake."

The image of a scared boy being sent from the safety of his home into the den of a monster by his own parents appeared in Tanya's mind. She pictured the boy, fearful, tears in his eyes, the vision morphing into the man who now sat struggling at times to breathe in his hospital bed a few feet away. Tanya felt like the game board of her life, full of the conclusions she'd made and knowledge she kept, had just shifted, as if someone had removed a sheet that had covered another half of the board she didn't know existed. It didn't take away the black section of her childhood home, but there was now a path there explaining it.

Jim couldn't read Tanya's face, so he kept talking. "Your daddy and I have similar stories, and in fact, if it weren't for him, I sure wouldn't still be alive. Your daddy is who helped me get sober. He got me going to AA and all that."

Tanya's face softened and she smiled warmly at Jim. "Thank you, Jim. I had no idea." She reached out to give him a hug adding, "Do you think you could sit with him for a bit? I need to process this, and maybe even make some phone calls. I'm not the only one who should know this story."

✶✶✶

It had been three weeks since Audrey had discharged Albert home with his daughter. Her mind had been so invaded with new patients and new drama, that it took her a minute to place the name "Albert Stone" when the home nurse, Tami, called about admitting him to the Hospice House. His breathing was so labored from the buildup of fluid from his heart failure, that he was requiring extensive morphine. Tami felt being able to give him intravenous morphine at the Hospice House would help. Audrey agreed.

Recalling the interaction with Albert and Tanya at the hospital was the salve Audrey needed after being beaten down by a difficult patient earlier in the day. It was rare to walk into a room to admit a patient and already have a relationship with them. Audrey found she was eager to see how Albert was doing and bounced down the hall to room 15 to welcome him.

A cacophony of sound bombarded Audrey as she neared the room. She frowned and turned to find a nurse or aide to confirm this was Albert's room before she blindly entered.

The room was packed with people, Audrey quickly scanned and guessed there were 15 people lining the walls and sitting on every available space.

"Albert!" she greeted warmly, as if they were old friends, and came near to his side. Physically he was much changed. His eyes were sunken, and his muscles wasted away. The oxygen streamed from a plastic face mask strapped around his face, which Albert held, pulling it away from his mouth to talk from time to time. The way he sank into the pillows supporting his sitting posture, Audrey guessed his strength was almost nonexistent.

Albert winked at Audrey, "Hiya, Doc."

Audrey could not hide her surprise as she glanced at all the faces encircling Albert. A toddler clung to a man's leg, two teenage boys huddled together peering at an iPad, a baby was snuggled in Tanya's arm. "You'll have to introduce me to all these people, Albert."

Despite how much effort the introductions would make, Albert clearly wanted this role. He slid the face mask to his chin and started with Tanya on his right. When Tanya and Audrey locked eyes a spark flew up Audrey's spine, was that peace she read in her gaze?

One by one he introduced the room: Grandchildren, his youngest son, Grant, and his wife, Tanya's husband, and a nephew and his family. As they went around the room, nodding at each other, Audrey's body shifted counterclockwise. Finally, they were to a gentleman standing next to Audrey.

Albert broke down in tears looking at the sharply dressed man next to Audrey. He wore glasses and a well-trimmed beard. His skin was tanned and wrinkled from work outdoors. She saw a rim of tears lining his lower eyelids but contained.

Gradually, Albert collected himself, "… and this is Teddy, my oldest boy." Audrey's heart swelled, threatening to burst from its boundaries as she reached out and shook Teddy's rough strong hands.

They spoke of symptoms and medications and of the reality of what loomed ahead in the next few days. Through it all, Albert nodded, a smile plastered on his face. Finally, Albert interrupted Audrey's teaching, "No offense Doc, but I really am okay, and I know what's coming. But you see, I've got twenty years of stories to get caught up on." Albert was too kind hearted to actually say, leave, but Audrey got the message.

She felt slightly self-conscious that she'd stayed so long. Outside of the room a crescendo of speech and then laughter spilled into the hallway. Audrey tried to bottle up the sound into her memory to be used later as needed and strode off to another room.

12. MARSHMALLOW

Linda

Audrey turned off her car, and reached over to the passenger side seat to grab her faux red leather satchel. As she stepped out of her maroon Jeep Grand Cherokee, she locked the car, threw the keys into the satchel and retrieved her name badge. She was parked in the back of the Hospice House.

The 30-foot walk to the back entrance was like a sci-fi transition zone to Audrey. She felt herself mentally put on a second skin. For the next eight hours she would be Dr. Audrey Clark, empathetic, present, and a channel for the fears and grieving of her patients and families. At least this is what she wanted to believe. In truth, she thought, this would be another day full of mundane moments, difficult conversations, and longing to get done with work so she could go home to her husband and

2-year-old daughter.

She greeted staff cheerfully as she made her way to her cubicle that she shared in a room of other hospice staff. The fate of her day would lie in a printed excel spreadsheet on her desk. The paper listed each room at the Hospice House, along with the patient occupying the room, their diagnosis, and which nurse was assigned to them.

Audrey sat, took out her lap top and cord from her satchel to plug in and turn on, and then picked up the paper to pour over the details. She had been present when Frank had passed yesterday afternoon and was expecting to see a blank line for room 17.

"What?" Audrey said out loud to no one, "They've already filled room 17 with a new admit? I wonder when this new lady came in." Audrey noted the details: Linda, age 39, Hepatocellular Carcinoma, Hep C, Liver Failure.

Audrey could not help starting a speculative narrative for the new patient, guessing she would find someone with previous substance abuse problems and little family support.

Audrey reached once more into her satchel to sling her stethoscope around her neck; it was time to get to work.

At the nurses' station, Audrey grabbed the new patient's chart, thumbing through outside records, meanwhile asking Victoria, the nurse working in Pod B, for the story.

"Linda came in from the home team around 10 p.m.," Victoria glanced down at her check-out notes. "They said she was having acute delirium and the family couldn't control her anymore. Dr. Calando gave them an order for Haldol last night, which seems to be working well."

Victoria was in her 40's and reminded Audrey of someone who would have been a hippie had she had the chance. Victoria had been a hospice nurse for 15 years and had a keen ability to connect with patients. Victoria's green eyes clouded with concern.

"It's actually a very sad case. Linda's husband Allen has already left for work, but their son, Toby is in there. Poor kid."

Audrey nodded and closed the chart, "I'm going to go meet her first, and then I'll catch up on the other patients."

It was hard not to think of recent patients, whose spirits seemed to still haunt the space of the rooms they had occupied. Outside of room 17, Audrey thought of Frank, the WWII vet who had died in this same room Linda now occupied. He'd been such a courageous man, able to find peace with his past before he died. What challenges and work would this young woman present?

Inside the room, Audrey noted an element of chaos. Linda was in a chair by the window, sitting up, yet groggy. Her long brown hair was unkempt and stringy. Her skin was a sunflower yellow from the liver failure. Her eyes were closed, and oxygen tubing lay discarded over one shoulder. The upper half of her body was thin, but starting just below her ribs, her belly bulged out like a woman in her 9th month of pregnancy. That same swelling was in her legs, giving them a tree trunk appearance, with tight skin that looked to be on the verge of splitting open.

There were trash and household items littering the area around her chair and bedside table, and on the bed sat a boy who appeared half child and half teenager. The boy had sandy colored hair, brown eyes and a remnant of freckles across his cheekbones. He immediately smiled in a self-assured way at Audrey.

"Hello, I'm Dr. Clark." Audrey addressed the boy first, unsure if Linda was awake. With the noise, Linda startled and opened her eyes halfway. It didn't appear she was focused on anything and quickly returned to her stupor.

"I'm Toby," the boy said, "and this is my mom. She'll wake up if you need her to." Toby was clearly comfortable with the situation and before Audrey could say otherwise, Toby leaned towards his mom and patted her arm.

"Hey Mom, the doctor's here." Linda flung her arm, shooing Toby away and gave a grunt in annoyance. Toby looked at Audrey masking any hurt with nonchalance.

"She hasn't really been herself in several weeks," he said. "She seems upset when my dad or I try to help her."

"How long has your mom been sick?"

Toby squished up his face in concentration, "Uh, hmm, let's see, maybe 2 years?"

"That's a long time." Audrey looked back at Linda in silence, contemplating what two years of sickness looked like for Toby.

"It's not really been too bad, until last month when we got hospice."

"What made you come into the Hospice House last night?" Audrey wasn't sure if Toby would have a sense of what pulled the trigger for admitting his mom; therefore, it surprised her when he answered.

"You see, she's been getting up a lot at night. She wants to walk up and down our stairs at home. She needs help, because she's unsteady. Night before last, I was up all night with her. I counted that we went up and down the stairs 20 times. My dad said we can't keep doing that, so the home hospice nurse told us to come in here." There was not one hint of pain in his statement, though Audrey's eyes had widened with this account.

"You walked her up and down the stairs all night?"

Toby was matter of fact and even shrugged when he said, "Yeah. She couldn't sit still or sleep, so that's what we did."

Linda stirred in her chair, and her eyes fluttered open. This time she seemed to focus on her surroundings.

"Linda? Hi, I'm Dr. Clark. I'm going to be taking care of you here."

Linda nodded then spoke, her words strung together without breaks, "I'm thirsty, can I have a drink?"

"Sure. I'll get you some water. Before I do, how are you feeling this morning?"

"Miserable. I need to get up." Linda used her arms to push on her chair in an attempt to rise, lifting herself 2 inches and then collapsed back into the chair. She made this same motion three more times, and realized it was fruitless, and sank back into a stupor.

"Hey, Dr. Clark," Toby rose and walked over to a backpack with Spiderman on the outside, "Is there a microwave in this room? I want to pop this marshmallow popcorn." Toby's face lit up as he looked at the image on the plastic bag.

"They make marshmallow popcorn?" Dr. Clark had internally decided that most of the productive work would need to be with Toby, as Linda seemed past the point of doing inner work.

Toby eagerly came to show Audrey the bag, "See? It's my favorite."

"Interesting! No microwave in here, but I'll show you where one is that you can use." As an afterthought she added, "Toby, when will your dad be back from work?"

"Oh, he didn't go to work today. He said he just was going home to take a nap and shower. He'll be back by lunch." This triggered some type of pleasant thought, as Toby's face lit up again, "He said you guys feed us here for free! Is that true?"

Audrey smiled and rose from her chair, mimicking Toby's enthusiasm, "Yes, they feed us all for free! C'mon, let's go pop some popcorn."

***

It was after lunch and Audrey sat in her cubicle entering notes on her computer from her patient visits. She had finished dictating Linda's History and Physical and decided to see if Linda's husband, Allen had arrived. Audrey had a foreboding feeling that Linda didn't have long to live.

Back at pod B, Audrey paused to get medical updates from Victoria.

"The Haldol does seem to work when she starts getting restless, but she's not been too coherent for me."

"What about Allen, is he here?"

An undecipherable look passed on Victoria's face. "He is." She appeared like she wanted to say more but stopped herself. Victoria tried hard to not bias others with her initial thoughts. This was admirable, Audrey thought, but it sure would be quicker, and sometimes easier, to be biased.

Inside the room, Linda had moved and was sitting on the edge of her bed. A stocky, shorter man with balding hair sat next to her, arm draped around her shoulders. Toby sat across the room in a chair reading "Diary of a Wimpy Kid" his right leg swinging rapidly up and down. Toby immediately put his book down and grinned at Audrey.

"The lunch here was great! Oh, and Dr. Clark, this is my dad, Allen." The man on the bed glanced over his shoulder at Audrey, his eyes puffy from crying.

Coming around to face Linda and Allen, Audrey saw that Linda was unchanged in appearance. Her eyes still closed, she was speaking at random times about things that didn't make sense.

"Take those clothes... milk and...snow on the trees...don't

you dare!" Linda's voice rose, speaking to no one in particular. Allen let out a little whimper, "Sweetie, what are you trying to say? I'm here, baby." Allen took his free hand and grasped his wife's hand.

Linda immediately shook both his hand and his arm draped around her, off, like shooing away a fly.

"Don't you touch me!" Linda's voice was stern. Toby, wanting to pacify the moment, came across and knelt before his mom.

"Hey, Mom, I love you." His voice was sincere and sweet.

"Well, I hate you!" Linda announced this, though speaking more to the air than to her son, the words clearly still cut Toby.

With maturity well beyond his years, he returned the volley, "I still love you anyways."

"Toby, could you do me a big favor?" Audrey wanted to be able to talk to Allen alone and concocted a quick distraction.

"Sure." Toby was eager to be helpful.

"I saw they put some fresh cookies out at the kitchen, could you go grab a plate and pick 6 or 7 cookies for you and your dad. Also, let's give one to your nurse, Victoria. She loves cookies!"

The task was just what Toby needed, and he left quickly.

Audrey spent the next few minutes talking through Linda's current condition with Allen. He struck Audrey as fragile. He cried through their talk, but his grief was almost panicky.

"I just don't know what I'm going to do!" He sobbed. "It's all changed so fast." Allen's two hands cupped his face, shielding him from Audrey. His grief, Audrey realized was acting just as his hands; a barrier, keeping him stuck and unable to talk about anything further. Linda meanwhile seemed oblivious, her lips continually moving, mouthing unintelligible words to no one.

Toby returned with his plate of cookies, eyes sparkling. "I gave most of them away to all the nurses I could find. I saved two though, for you guys."

Audrey grabbed a cookie and prepared to leave, resting a hand on Toby's shoulder she concluded, "You are a spectacular young man, Toby. Any parent would be lucky to have you as their son."

✲✲✲

The following morning, Audrey was eager to check in on Linda and her family. However, with no new patients to visit, she decided to see her least complicated patients first. Get the easy ones done, that way I can pour my remaining energy into the difficult ones, Audrey thought.

It was midmorning when she was finally ready for Linda. Victoria was working again and filled Audrey in on the changes.

"She's transitioned now and is actively dying," Victoria stated, "some mottling on her feet, periods of apnea. She had some secretions last night while breathing. I don't think the family got much sleep."

Audrey made mental notes as Victoria spoke of what things she'd need to explain to Allen and Toby.

As she entered Linda's room the atmosphere felt denser from the sadness. Allen sat huddled in a chair on one side of Linda's bed, hands raised and cupping his head again. Toby sat on the opposite side of the bed, both hands cradling his mother's hand. Linda, still bright yellow, had her eyes closed and was propped at a 30-degree angle in the bed. Her mouth, relaxed, hung slightly open, her breathing spaced with long pauses.

Toby attempted a small smile at Audrey, while Allen stayed isolated in his tearful cocoon. Audrey squatted down parallel to Toby and swiped her hand across the top of his back.

"I just kept thinking last night that she was going to die." Toby let a few tears spill out of his eyes. "I was so tired. I'd fall asleep and then get scared and wake up and think she was gone." Audrey let him cry for a bit, knowing there were no words that could take away his pain.

He settled and then turned away from his mom and asked, "Dr. Clark, what's wrong with my mom's feet and legs?"

Audrey nodded, "Yes, I wanted to talk to you about that." She moved very tenderly to the foot of the bed and carefully pulled up one side of the sheet, making sure not to reveal too much skin. Linda's exposed leg was still swollen with fluid but was dark blue now up to her knee. Her toes were the darkest, with a splotchy bruising appearance the further up you went. Allen briefly took his hands down and looked over to his wife's leg. The sight was too much for him, and he retreated again. Toby, on the other hand had a mixture of worry and curiosity on his face.

"This is something called mottling." Audrey placed a hand on Linda's shin and then cupped her toes gently. "It doesn't hurt her, and you can feel where the purple part is, it's very cold."

Toby timidly reached his hand out to touch his mom's ankle. As soon as he made contact his hand flew back, as if he had been burned, and then reached out again.

"Wow! That is so cold!" The inquisitive child part of Toby was momentarily disassociating from what reality was.

"What this tells us," Audrey explained, "is that your mom's heart is not doing a good job pumping her blood right now. Her toes are the farthest away from her heart, so that's why they are the coldest and the most purple."

"Ah," Toby said with new understanding. Audrey watched Toby's body language as the information slowly seeped in and he connected the dots.

His shoulders sagged, "So she is going to die soon." In the background, Allen's whole body shook as he cried in great big gulps.

Audrey came back to Toby's side and simply said, "I'm so sorry."

"Can she still hear us?"

"Toby, that's one of those things I have to believe is true."

"Because, I've been telling her not to go." With this Toby broke down. He put his head into his arms which rested to the side of his mother and cried.

Audrey looked over at Allen who was in his own bitter sadness. A kernel of anger popped within Audrey, as she longed for this father to come and comfort his son. Audrey settled her hand on Toby's back, but professionalism restricted her from wrapping him in a motherly hug. Tears filled Audrey's eyes and she felt the desperation of life's unfairness.

Intuition told Audrey she'd been in the room long enough. With a final pat on Toby's back she exited the room, sure that this heavy cloud of melancholy would follow her the rest of the day.

✳✳✳

Audrey hadn't been on call the night before which meant phone calls about anyone who passed away in the night went to Audrey's partner, Dr. Calando. She felt guilty, realizing that she hoped that Linda had died in the night. Audrey wasn't sure she could emotionally repeat yesterday.

When she saw the list for the day on her desk, and an empty room 17, her reprieve was quickly tempered by thoughts of Toby. In fact, though not physically present, Audrey was surprised that she carried Toby around with her through the day. She knew the social worker and bereavement team would be following closely, but her mind still wandered.

✷✷✷

The following day, Audrey could tell Toby was already beginning to recede from her thoughts. They taught this in medical school, Audrey rationalized, and I must let these families go to be an effective Doctor. Audrey's inner dialogue continued as she made her way past room 17, and the new patient, Terrence, who had been admitted into that room yesterday.

Audrey's thoughts were abruptly cut off when she came to the nurses' station and saw Victoria sitting, tears and anguish on her face. T'Neek and Michelle, two of the aides, stood frozen with hands over their open mouths and eyes wide in horror.

Audrey's heart palpated with fear, "What? What is going on?"

Victoria tried to get the information out through multiple stops and starts.

"I just got off the phone with...with...with the home team."

"...and," Audrey was impatient to hear what could be causing this much alarm.

"Allen." Victoria paused and then more crying, "Toby." She couldn't spit it out and Audrey hearing those names felt time slow down infinitely.

Finally, T'Neek jumped in, "Last night Allen took some, or actually a lot, of Linda's prescription pain pills that were still in the house. I guess because he couldn't sleep."

Michelle finished, "Toby found him this morning. It was an overdose, he's gone."

Audrey felt as if she'd been kicked in the gut. Every fiber of her body wanted to scream out at the top of her lungs, "NO!" But instead, the shock kept any actual words from forming. She just shook her head, over and over again, back and forth, no.

Suddenly Audrey turned and half ran back down the hall. In the same way someone runs to a bathroom when their stomach shouts that food is getting ready to be expelled, Audrey felt she was about to vomit up her emotions.

Audrey burst through the doors of the circular chapel in the middle of the Hospice House. She collapsed into one of the chairs, choking on her sobs that spewed out the moment she crossed the threshold into that peaceful and private space.

The thoughts erupted and poured down over her one by one.

Why?

So selfish!

Should I have seen this coming?

What if?

Toby, dear God, Toby!

This isn't real, is it? This must be a nightmare!

Audrey's heart felt as if a vice grip had been applied; there was a physical tightness just beneath her ribs. Her mind raced for some sort of solution to latch onto. Maybe she could adopt Toby? She tried to insert Toby into visions of her home and family, only to realize how improbable that would be.

A nagging voice in her head reminded her she had patients to see. She understood that this grief was too large to carry around with her today or any other day. Doing what most people would find callous, but essential to survive as a palliative care doctor, Audrey mentally wrapped a large burlap tarp around all her angst, around Toby and Allen and Linda, around the questions and doubts and sadness. She visualized pulling up the corners to contain the miasma and tying it up into a giant sack with heavy rope and sealing it. She then imagined putting the bag away. For another time, she thought.

She then sat up straight and wiped the last tears away under her eyes. She took some deep breaths and just sat in a moment void of thoughts.

When it was time, she readjusted the stethoscope around her neck and ran her thumb across her name badge. She stood shaking her arms and hands, as if flinging dirt away, and with pretend confidence, she pushed open the chapel door and headed back to work.

13. DEFIANCE

Kyanna

Anise stepped out of her daughter's hospice room. Pushing against her coat pocket, she felt for the familiar square carton edges and round protruding lighter. As she walked past the small visitor's kitchen, a strange smell caught her attention. She turned towards the scent and saw a young teenage boy tearing open a fresh bag of popcorn. She couldn't place the sweet smell intermixed with the familiar popcorn aroma. The boy caught her inquisitive stare and beamed, "You want some? It's coated with marshmallows."

Anise was caught off guard by his friendliness. "Thanks sweetie, but it's too early for me." She continued her path to the nearest door out to the expansive gardens in the center of the Hospice House.

It was chilly, and Anise huddled her shoulders inward as she pulled her cigarette and lighter out. The boy's innocent smile lingered in her mind's eye as she drew deeply on the cigarette. She guessed he was close to her grandson Carl's age. A pang of grief surged with the thought. Her mind wandered down a well-trodden path.

She tried to picture what Carl would look like at 14 years of age. She imagined him with his mother's dark brown eyes and black hair. It had been ten years since she'd seen him. The ornery spark she witnessed when he was four was certainly still there. She closed her eyes, making her daydream more vivid. She imagined him in a football uniform, sitting in a class answering questions, and introducing a pretty girlfriend, all awkward and shy. She felt herself smiling, and her eyes snapped open, self-conscious that someone might have seen her. But she was alone on the cement patio, facing the center of the gardens.

Her dreams, though bright on the inside, were always encircled by darkness. Was he truly okay, she wondered? Had he been adopted or was he still in the foster system? Her smile turned downward quickly, and self-hatred took root. If only she had interceded. If Carl's mother, her own daughter, couldn't protect him, she at least as his grandmother, should have. Her insides burned with regret. The lines of her face shriveled deeper and muscles tightened as she ground her spent cigarette into the cement. And now this, her daughter was dying of cancer. She silently shook her head in disgust at how life had turned out and turned to go back inside.

She didn't look for the popcorn boy but made a bee-line for Room 12. She entered the room gruffly. She'd given up being quiet. It didn't seem to matter. Her daughter, Kyanna, lay on her back and looked like she was sleeping. She spoke to Kyanna as she dropped onto the couch, "I don't know what you are waiting for."

There was no response, just as there had been no response for days. The first two weeks they'd been at the Hospice House had been hell. Kyanna was delirious and screaming. She even stood up on her hospital bed one night shouting "Help!" before collapsing in weakness into a crumpled mess back on the bed. The Doctor had worked tirelessly increasing medications, trying to help the transition. Finally, she calmed, or was on enough medication that she seemed calm. Anise chuckled to herself thinking how a week ago, when Kyanna had finally settled, that everyone had assumed she only had a day or two left to live.

Anise heard the tap on the door just before Dr. Audrey Clark stepped in. Audrey gave a sheepish smile, greeting Anise, "I see you are still here."

"She's just the same as yesterday, and the day before, and the day before that."

Audrey took in Anise's annoyed tone and apologized, "I don't know what to tell you." Audrey made her way to Kyanna and did her exam. There was no response, no movement save the slow rise and fall of her chest. Audrey crossed to Anise and shared the couch with her.

"Isn't there something we can do? I hate just waiting. Why is it taking so long?"

Audrey looked sympathetic, "Believe it or not, she seems comfortable. She's just not ready yet."

"C'mon, you think this is her hanging on?" Anise was skeptical.

"Possibly," Audrey answered, "I don't really have other explanations. She hasn't had anything to eat in, what, three weeks?" Anise nodded. Audrey continued, "And nothing to drink in a

week, right?" Again, Anise affirmed the information. "The aver-
age is two weeks for nutrition and hydration, and as you see she's
well past that. It makes me think there's something else going on
in there."

"So that's it? There's nothing to do?"

Audrey had debated whether to bring up her last-ditch idea,
but sensing the extreme frustration, she decided to go for it.
"Well, it's a shot in the dark, but there's one thing you could try."

Anise looked eager, "Yes, please, anything!"

"There's this relatively famous Palliative Care doctor named
Ira Byock who wrote a book called, 'The Four Things that Matter
Most'. He says that as humans, there are certain things we need
to hear before we die. I like to add one more and make it the five
things that matter most."

"Things to say?" Anise asked, a puzzled expression on her
face.

"Right. I know it sounds hokey, but I've seen it make a difference. If nothing else, it usually is powerful for the family itself."
Audrey added, "It's not easy, but if you want to try everything,
you may want to try this."

Anise sighed unsure what she thought about all this. "Okay.
Hit me. What are the magic words?"

"No, no. Not magic." Audrey decided to change her approach, "Look, clearly your daughter has not been at peace. We
all watched her go through such a rough transition, which usually points to something she's wrestling with. It may be she is hoping for something from you; absolution, gratitude, or perhaps
even permission." Audrey believed in this idea wholeheartedly
but knew many people didn't like to deal with these intangible
things. She could see Anise had buy-in now, so she finished,
"The four things are, 'Forgive me,' 'I forgive you,' 'Thank you,'

and 'I love you.' The fifth thing can be hard, but I think it's also important, 'Goodbye.'"

Audrey let the words soak in, and saw tears form on the lower lids of Anise's eyes. She concluded, "Think about it. It's asking a lot, I know. But it just may be that Kyanna needs to hear one of those things."

Anise nodded, but didn't want to speak, for fear she'd start crying in earnest. Audrey sensed the conversation was over and patted Anise's knee as she rose and left the room. Outside the door, Audrey inhaled slowly. She wished for the hundredth time that Kyanna would give up the struggle and go. If it was challenging for Audrey to come in daily and see the lifeless 32-year-old just lying there, she couldn't imagine how hard it was for Anise to sit, day after day, waiting.

Back in the room, Anise struggled to keep her composure. She wasn't sure she could do it. She was aware that her time alone with Kyanna would be ending within the hour, when Anise's two sisters arrived, so she heaved herself up and fought her way through her resistance to the side of Kyanna's bed. She looked at her daughter, gaunt and emaciated. The luster was absent from the short spiked new black hair that had grown back after chemo, and there were dark circles surrounding her eyes. Her mouth gaped open, revealing her chipped and rotting teeth. Anise reached for her daughter's left arm and ran her own hand down the length of Kyanna's arm, pausing over old track mark scars. Tears began to drip onto the bed.

"You know I love you, Kyanna," Anise's voice was hesitant and soft, "and I'm so thankful for you. My parents may not have been so thankful; me at 16 years of age and pregnant, but you and me, we were two peas in a pod." Anise smiled and looked up at her daughter's waxy face, looking for any sign she heard.

There was nothing. Anise continued, "If only I could have kept you away from…" Anise choked on the name, uttering it with venom, "Jax."

"Oh God, you were only 14. Why did I think it was okay that a nineteen-year-old wanted to go out with you?" Anise sobbed, "I saw all the signs, the bruises, coming home high, dropping out of school, and yet, I just let it all happen." Anise lay her forehead down against Kyanna's upturned palm. The clammy, cool feeling was hardly noticed by Anise, who continued after some moments of tears.

"If only I could have stopped it, then Carl might still be with us." A knife-like feeling seared through Anise's heart, "I know you think it was your fault, and that the courts said you were responsible. But I'm your mother, and I know that it was Jax who corrupted you, getting you hooked on Heroin. And that after all those years of abuse, you couldn't say no to him." Anise looked again at her daughter's face as she said mournfully, "I hope you know that I forgive you."

The tide had been loosed, and Anise let the words spill out into the room. "If you had been clear headed, I know you wouldn't have let Jax do those horrible things to Carl. I know you would have stopped him…"

Images that Anise had worked years to keep out of her brain darted across her mind. It was Anise who had gone over that Saturday, eleven years ago. Anise hadn't seen her daughter and grandson for over six months and had lost track of where they were living. A friend of a friend tipped Anise off that they were staying in a small two room foreclosed home in a rundown part of town.

She recalls walking into the dilapidated house. Several windows were out, garbage and abandoned junk were strewn on the un-mowed yard. She announced herself as she entered. Clearly there was no electricity and the putrid stench was suffocating. Broken glass crunched underneath her feet, and a faint glow of a candle in the back room gave her the courage to keep walking into the house. She passed more trash and had to cover her mouth to keep from vomiting as she passed a bucket used as a latrine with used pieces of toilet paper scattered nearby.

Nothing prepared her, however, for the candle lit room. A sleeping bag on top of an old mattress was pushed against the corner and her daughter half sat, half fell against the wall. Her mouth hung open, a string of drool hung by the side of her mouth. Kyanna's eyes were half open, pupils pinpoint and blank. The band used to tie off her arm lay on her lap, and a used needle sat next to the candle, foil, and pouch of powdered Heroin. She had called out in fright and anger for Kyanna to wake up, demanding to know where Carl was. Kyanna batted her mother away and toppled over onto the bed.

It was then that Anise heard a small whimper and turned to the open door across the room. In the door frame of what had been the bathroom of the house, she saw the dog cage. It stood two and a half feet tall, and she shrieked when she saw a small hand gripping one of the bars.

"Carl!" She squealed, diving at the door of the cage and fumbling to open it. The cage reeked of feces and urine. The three-year-old boy didn't move, even with the door open. He sat on his knees in a pull up, his eyes wide and fearful. The image of him sitting in squalor and that hollow expression on his face was seared into her consciousness even now.

Tears plummeted down Anise's cheeks. "I'm the one to blame for what that monster did to Carl." Anise couldn't look at Kyanna for the next part. She felt her heart twisted in knots of emotion and she closed her eyes pleading, "Will you forgive me, Kyanna?"

She knew internally she'd never forgive herself, and didn't feel she deserved forgiveness from Kyanna, but if it helped her daughter find peace, she wanted to try.

"I tried so hard to make it up to you. I thought maybe, if I could help you beat this cancer..." Anise's head dropped, crushed by the memories of the past year and a half. The countless doctors' appointments, car rides to treatment, hospital stays, cleaning up vomit and urine, and giving medications. Whatever Kyanna asked for or demanded Anise had been there. But she'd failed again.

After some time, Anise opened her eyes, but wasn't ready to look at Kyanna's face. Instead she stared at the rhythm of her breathing. Slow and steady. She spoke more confidently now, "As for the last thing, it isn't so hard to say." She paused and then raised her gaze to the half open, blank stare of her daughter. "Goodbye, sweetie. You've suffered long enough."

Anise squeezed her daughter's arm and examined her face for any small indication of change. Seeing only the stillness, she looked again to her chest and the rise and fall. She waited expectantly, willing it to slow or stop, but it carried on, the same as before. Defeated and exhausted, Anise rose and collapsed back into the couch.

✶✶✶

Four more days passed, and Audrey had to force herself to enter Room 12. She hated the way Kyanna's family looked at her, eager to hear news of some type of change. Whereas, elsewhere, the report of death was received as bad news, in this room it would be reason to celebrate. The pleaser in Audrey felt like she was disappointing the family when she verbalized that Kyanna would live another day.

Please let there be something different today, Audrey prayed, as she entered the room. The room had the smell of death, as it had for days. Anise and her two sisters sat in their typical places. Audrey found it hard to even smile at them, sensing their pain.

She went to Kyanna and began her exam. Her eyes were opened widely, crust matted on the edges and redness from not being able to blink any longer. Her gaze was fixed upward. Audrey took out her pin light and flashed it in a back and forth motion over Kyanna's eyes. The pupils were dilated but still had a very slight response to the light. The tip of Kyanna's nose was purple, as was the skin around her open mouth. The way Kyanna rested on the pillow looked uncomfortable, her chin jutting up towards the ceiling, leaving her neck looking overly long and rigid. The nurses had tried to readjust, but it was as if her neck was stuck in this position.

Audrey noted Kyanna's breathing was shallow, and the stethoscope revealed a faint thread of a heartbeat. Her ribs could be seen through the hospice gown, and her lower abdomen sank down at least two inches from her chest. Audrey listened to her bowels not expecting to hear anything, as it had been 35 days since she'd eaten anything.

Moving down the body, Audrey carefully lifted the side of the sheet to look at Kyanna's knees and legs. She saw the familiar mottling of her knee caps but was then startled to see something new. There along the back of Kyanna's thigh, leading into her buttocks was a deep purple solid color. It was as if someone had dipped that part of her body into a vat of purple dye.

"Well, this is new," Audrey stated. Anise immediately jumped over to Audrey's side, excited for something different. Audrey touched the skin, and felt the rigid firm area, "Huh," she said in disbelief.

"What is it?" Anise asked.

"It's something called liver mortis," Audrey said incredulously, "it's blood pooling back here in her tissues." Audrey looked back again at Kyanna's chest, making sure she really was still breathing. The ladies waited for more explanation, and Audrey filled them in, "I've just never seen this on someone who was living. This is what happens after the body dies."

This insight seemed to unhinge something within Anise, "We've had enough," she sobbed, making her way to the head of the bed. Anise put her hand on her daughter's forehead and the other two women came near the bed.

"You listen to me, Kyanna," Anise commanded, "I have been patient. I have sat here, by your side, day after day, but this is too much. I am suffering here. It is miserable, it's like I'm trapped in this room, in a never-ending nightmare." Anise's sisters echoed her remarks with similar sentiments, which added to the frenzied mood.

"Your body is done, it is basically dead. Why won't you go?" Anise lowered herself so that her elbows rested on the side of the mattress and her two hands were clasped in a pleading manner.

Her words became chant like, "Don't you see Jesus? He's waiting for you! You just need to go to him, go. It's time you go, go!" Audrey began to back away from the bed as the volume increased. Anise was desperate and she begged with anguish.

'Please go, go now!' echoed from the three women one after another. Audrey tried hard not to pity them. Audrey felt herself saying the words in her head, "Yes, go. Please, just go."

Suddenly a hideous sound erupted, a guttural, barely intelligible, yet startlingly forceful, "No!" thundered out of Kyanna's lifeless body.

The hair on the back of Audrey's neck stood to attention, and the room was momentarily ushered into profound silence. Looks of shock, mixed with horror, passed between all of them. The three sisters turned to Audrey daring her to explain what just happened.

Audrey shook her head silently and shrugged her shoulders. "Whatever shred of control Kyanna has in this process, she clearly is exercising. There's nothing else to say. She's not ready to go. I don't know why she's not ready, but this is her sheer will at this point. "

Anise, of course, knew. The reverberations of Kyanna's shout echoed in Anise's ears. The torment her daughter must be struggling with descended as an anchor into the pit of her chest and Anise let her face fall into the bed, encircling her head with her arms. In that cocoon of darkness, she wept.

14. VERDICT

Mimi

Reverend Anita Charles hung up the office phone and let out a deep, weary sigh. Her fingers massaged her temples as she bent her head towards her desk and closed her eyes. "Lord, here we go again," she said quietly and tried to let her mind rest.

"Reverend," the timid voice of Anita's secretary at Grace African Methodist Episcopal Church called, standing in the doorway to Anita's office, "are you okay?"

Looking up and moving her hands back to her note strewn desk, Anita replied, "Yes, Sarah. Sorry, I was just collecting my thoughts. That was the hospital. They admitted Mom from the nursing home again. They think pneumonia or urine infection is most likely."

"Wasn't she just there?"

Another sigh escaped Anita, "Yes. Yes, got out four days ago. I think this is the sixth time she's been in this year."

"Can I do anything to help?"

Anita began to shake her head no, but then stopped, "Actually, would you reschedule my 2 o'clock meeting with Franklin. I really should head up to the hospital this afternoon."

"Absolutely," Sarah said, retreating to her desk situated outside Anita's office. Anita looked down at her desk. Several Bible commentaries were open, and the notes for this Sunday's sermon suddenly seemed foreign. Her eyes wandered to a framed photograph on the right corner of her desk. It was the last family photo taken before her father had died suddenly of a heart attack 15 years prior.

In the photo, Carl and Mimi Andover sat in two large velvet chairs wearing their Sunday best. Carl's hefty body dwarfed Mimi's slight one. On Mimi's head, she wore her favorite church hat. It had a wide black brim, a folded fabric flower to the side with six dainty feathers sprouting from the flower's edge. When Mimi was in her 20's she had developed Vitiligo, an autoimmune disorder that causes patches of skin to turn white. The contrast of Mimi's dark ebony skin littered with several white areas around her mouth, nose, and forehead gave her the appearance of a calico cat. Pressed together, surrounding the two chairs were the children: Anthony, Bobby, James, Anita, Helen, and Junior. Everyone seemed happy. Anita smiled as she remembered that day, her ordination day. Her eyes moistened as she focused on Mimi. In many ways, Anita felt like the woman in the picture was already gone.

Mimi started having problems forgetting things nearly a decade ago. Initially, it was more annoyance, as she would repeat the same story several times. During that period, all of Mimi's children still lived within 20 miles of Mimi's home; therefore, many of the signs of dementia escaped them, likely because of the constant barrage of the family's helpful presence and all.

It was five years ago that it became clear that Mimi was not okay. She had wandered out of her home one night, in her nightgown of all things. The overnight clerk at the convenience store three blocks down happened to be the boyfriend of one of Anita's nieces. He called the family and averted a crisis. Within that next year, they placed her in a nursing home.

The last real conversation Anita had with her mother was two years ago, if you could call it a conversation. Mimi had not recognized her children for months, and though Anita came to the rest home to share a meal every Friday, Mimi referred to Anita generically as "sweet child." Her speech had become hard to understand, but that day as Anita helped spoon mashed potatoes into her mother's mouth, Mimi had reached her hand over to Anita's forearm, squeezed it, and said clearly, "Nita child, you keep this family together." Anita was a single woman with no children. Besides her church life, she devoted herself to her mother, so this request made sense. As Anita thought back to that moment, she shuddered to think that her Mother might have known she was slipping into the oblivion of dementia.

With effort, Anita pulled herself from the memory. She was not the oldest, but the family had placed her in charge. She rubbed her temple again and picked up the phone. She had quite a few phone calls to make to her family, and she was not looking forward to it.

✳✳✳

It was half past three when Anita walked into the entrance at

The University of Kansas Hospital. She was very familiar with the hospital, as she often made pastoral visits to hospitalized church members.

Anthony, the oldest at 65, along with his wife Kitty, as well as Junior, the youngest at 55, and his wife Shona, were already in room 408 of unit 43 in the hospital. Mimi lay in the hospital bed sleeping deeply. She had a facemask with oxygen on, and Anita saw an I.V. bag hanging in the corner, hooked up to a bandaged area with a needle in Mimi's left arm. The right arm had several bandages on it as well, and Anita knew that meant it had been hard to find a vein for the fluids.

"Nita," Anthony said, nodding his head in greeting. There were two chairs in the room, situated by the head of either side of the bed and both occupied by the sisters-in-law. Anita's brothers leaned against the one window in the room, resting on the narrow air conditioning unit beneath it. Anita took her place at the foot of the bed and reached to rub her mother's blanket covered feet.

"Mama, it's Nita." There was no response.

"The nurse said she may be skeptic," Junior started, interrupted by Anthony who was shaking his head.

"Not skeptic, septic! They have her on antibiotics and the fluids are to help bring her blood pressure up. It's pretty low."

Anita nodded at the information, staring at her mother's gaunt face and thin arms. She had always been petite, but now her small frame looked skeletal.

Junior, clearly not wanting to be left out added, "They also said something about her kidneys, maybe needing to do dial assist or something."

Anthony snorted and said mockingly, "Boy, where you grow up at? It's dialysis."

Kitty piped up chidingly, "Anthony, speak nicely to your brother."

"Dialysis! My, that would be pretty extreme," Anita voiced to the room, ignoring the brewing conflict.

"No, it would not be extreme. Nothing is extreme for our mama," Anthony spouted back.

The hospital room door opened, and Bobby and James bound in, treating the situation more like a party. "What's up brother?" Bobby announced coming over to give loud back slapping hugs to Anthony and Junior. James greeted Anita with a firm handshake before moving over to the men. The brothers stood now in a semi-circle, laughing and joking, the seriousness of their mother's health lost on them.

Over the next hour, family members came and went. At 5:30 p.m., Dr. Maisy Smith, Mimi's long-time physician, stopped in. Dr. Smith was Anita's age, 59, and they had both graduated high school together. She was tall and slender and carried herself with confidence. She was as much a family friend as physician.

After taking some moments to examine Mimi, Dr. Smith addressed the room, which was crowded with the 10 adults. "I know you realize that your mother is very sick. I want to remind you that in the past six months, she has been hospitalized six times. Each time she comes in, we have been aggressive, and we have patched her back up, best we can. But this is taking a toll on her body." Dr. Smith paused and looked around the room. Anita followed Dr. Smith's gaze, noting that a few of the brothers were nodding in agreement, while others appeared skeptical. "I need you to begin to discuss as a family what your limits are with your mother."

Junior piped up, "What do you mean limits?"

"When should we stop? If her kidneys shut down, would she

want dialysis? If she were not able to breathe on her own, would she want intubated? If she could not swallow, would she want a feeding tube? Those are the discussions you need to have."

The moment had a very solemn feel to it. Anthony spoke quickly in disbelief, "Those aren't really choices for us to make, now, are they? She's in a hospital to get better, so let's get her better!"

Kitty added, "That's right," and a few "Mmm hmms" echoed in support.

"The problem is, we can't actually make her better, Anthony," Anita quipped.

"What?" Anthony retorted, temper rising, "What is that supposed to mean? Of course she can get better; they are giving her medicine right now for that very purpose!"

The room erupted into several side conversations, the noise growing. Dr. Smith, tired from a long day in clinic, did not want to mediate this tonight. She cleared her throat and raised her right hand to quiet the room. "Excuse me." Conversations ceased and eyes drew back to Dr. Smith. "I can tell you have a lot to discuss and work through. For now, our course is set. Please take time to talk this out, and we can meet again tomorrow evening." As soon as her hand lowered, voices began again. Anita followed her out of the room.

"Well, I want to know what you think," Anita asked quietly out in the hall.

"Nita, your mom is really sick. We do have many things we can offer as her body fails, things that will keep her alive." Dr. Smith put her hand on Anita's upper arm and said empathically, "However, look at her Nita. She has no awareness whatsoever. She does not speak, she does not eat on her own, and she cannot walk. This is what the end of Alzheimer's looks like. I think all of these infections are her way of saying 'let me go.'"

Dr. Smith's candor surprised Anita, who said hesitatingly, "I'm not sure. I am going to need some time to process."

"Absolutely. Lead the family Nita; I know it's what your mother would have wanted." A nurse on the unit who was patiently waiting took this as a moment to interrupt. "I'm sorry Dr. Smith, but I needed to update you on what the husband decided for your patient in room 414."

Dr. Smith nodded and addressed Anita now as a friend, "What a day. I have a patient who came in yesterday as yellow as the sun, who had not been in a hospital for 20 years! We unfortunately just diagnosed her with cholangiocarcinoma. Contrast that with your mother who has practically lived in this hospital for the last 6 months. Everyone's journey is so different. I'd better go see what the plan is for her!" Dr. Smith gave her friend a hug and followed the nurse down the hall.

Anita did not move. The full weight of the day settled on her. She could hear her family arguing through the closed door. Noise, she thought, just angry noise. Anita did not want to go in and face their heated discussions. A verse from Isaiah came to her mind, "When you walk through the fire, you will not be scorched, nor will the flame burn you." As she pushed the door to enter back into the room, she smiled to herself thinking, "We shall just see if I don't get burned!"

***

When Anita finally crossed the threshold of her home, she walked to the couch and collapsed. It was 1 a.m., and Anita wanted only to sleep. The family had spent the last six hours hashing out opinions on those dicey decisions Dr. Smith wanted them to make. Initially they had hoped the discussion could be postponed a few weeks, but the night nurse had informed them that even if her pneumonia cleared, they'd still need to decide on a feeding tube or not.

Oh Mama, she thought, this is all your fault, raising strong-willed, independent children! Anita thought back to the raucous dinners of her childhood. Mimi always made fried chicken on Sundays, and after church, the family would gather round the table and debate politics and theology. Mimi would never join in, dismissing their verbal battles as foolishness. However, the twinkle in her eye, slight grin, and constant presence during their quarrels said otherwise.

Of course, none of this would be happening if Mimi had just written something down about her wishes. Anita searched her memory for anything her mother might have said about a situation like this. Nothing but memories of Mimi as a strong, no-nonsense matriarch came to mind. Anita exhaled slowly and willed her mind to rest. The last words she uttered before falling asleep were, "Sweet Jesus, help us all."

✳✳✳

The phone woke Anita from her fitful slumber. She reached toward the floor where her cell had dropped and saw her sister Helen's name as the caller. "It's about time," she muttered, noting to herself it was 7:30 a.m. as she answered.

The apologies started immediately, "Nita, I am so sorry. I got your message of course, but had meetings until eight, then had hours of research and a brief to write still. How is she, though, this morning?"

Helen was Anita's younger sister, and exuded ambition in everything she did. Currently she was a junior partner at a law firm on the east coast. Anita spent time updating Helen on Mimi's condition and explaining what the family had been tasked to decide.

"I am with Anthony on this one, Nita. We cannot give up on Mama already! I say whatever it takes, that's my vote anyway." This was not a surprise to Anita, especially as Helen had not actually been to visit their mother in over a year. Anita heard voices and commotion on the line. "Look, Nita, I have a meeting getting ready to start. I know you are mom's power of attorney, and the decision for all of this falls on you." Helen paused and her tone softened, "I guess I just wanted to say, good luck."

Tears came to Anita's eyes as she hung up. It was the first time anyone in the family had acknowledged the weight that she carried. The problem was she needed more than luck.

✶✶✶

As Anita walked the corridor outside of unit 43 she passed two nurses she recognized from the floor. They were deep in discussion and did not notice Anita. "They nearly got into a fist fight, and the poor woman, I wouldn't wish her existence on anyone!" Anita pondered what dysfunctional family the nurses were discussing as she entered unit 43. Her eyes immediately noted a commotion to the right side of the unit outside the room. It struck her all at once; it was in fact her own family causing the disturbance.

Anthony and his son Marcus stood squarely opposite Junior

and his son Miles. Anthony's face was rigid and angry, his finger up in an accusatory position towards Miles. Though still 40 feet away their voices were easily heard. "Look at her! You call that living?" Miles protested vehemently.

"So, you would just have us kill her, is that it?" spit flew from Anthony's lips. A nurse came and interrupted, "I need you to lower your voices. This is not an appropriate place for this."

Anita finally reached the group and apologized to the nurse for her family. "Please," she pleaded as the nurse walked away, "let's talk about this calmly. Can we at least go in the room to discuss this?"

"In front of her? Nita, it would traumatize her, maybe even kill her to overhear us talking about these things."

"She's not even coherent, Anthony!" Miles argued. Anita felt the tension and decided not to push things further.

"Nita, what are you going to do?" Junior timidly asked.

Anita frowned and her eyebrows knit together, "What do you mean?"

"Bobby said last night that all of this fighting was a waste of time, because you were the one who makes the decision."

"I can't believe this," Anthony growled and pushed past them all, exiting the unit. Anita sighed, her hand reflexively coming up to her temple as if in pain.

"No, Junior, this isn't my decision. Yes, technically I have the power to choose, but we are a family and should make these decisions together." The look on Anita's face was that of consternation.

Junior, always the tenderhearted one, reached over to give Anita a hug. As he did, he whispered in Anita's ear, "I think we should let her go."

∗∗∗

Late in the afternoon, Anita found herself alone in the room with her mother. Up until this moment, there were at least three people present at all times. Anita sat to her mother's left side in the stiff hospital room chair. Mimi still had on the facemask, and her eyes were closed. Her jaw, Anita noticed, seemed unnaturally open. She held her mother's frail hand in her palm, her other hand tracing the prominent tendons, veins, and bones of Mimi's hand. There was no indication that Mimi even felt Anita's touch. "Mama, this is so hard." Hearing her own agonized voice, tears began to spill onto Anita's cheeks. "We love you so much. I just don't know what we should do." Anita stared at her mother's face, willing some answer or indication to present itself. When none came, she sat up straight and wiped away her tears, a solution finally forming in her mind.

There was a knock on the door, and a nurse entered. "Are you Reverend Charles?" the nurse asked. Anita nodded and the nurse continued, "I am supposed to pass on that Dr. Smith plans to make rounds and meet with the family at 5:00 tonight." As an afterthought, she added, "And she did say she'd need a decision tonight on which way to take things." The nurse smiled sheepishly, undoubtedly fully aware of the impending chaos such a decision implied.

Anita looked up at the generic clock on the wall. She had just under two hours to get the word out to everyone about the meeting.

∗∗∗

Thankfully, Dr. Smith had reserved a conference room in the middle of Unit 43 for the family to meet. She arrived a few minutes late and when she entered the room, she thought maybe she had walked into the wrong place, as people packed the room. Anita saw Dr. Smith's look of bewilderment and quickly came to reassure her. "I know it's a lot, but this is all family, and they want to be a part of this decision." Dr. Smith did a very quick estimate and counted 35 people in the 20' by 20' room. Half of the family sat in a wide circle, while the other half stood directly behind on the perimeter of the room. Anita motioned to the only empty chair, seated directly next to hers.

Dr. Smith had everyone introduce himself or herself, mostly for her benefit. She knew a third of the family, but many of Anita's nieces and nephews she had not met. Dr. Smith updated everyone on Mimi's status and was very direct in saying that she was at a crossroad. She explained that there were two options at this point. One option was to acknowledge that Mimi's quality of life was at a point that would not be acceptable to her, and they would then simply allow a natural process to occur, without intervening any more. The other option was to intervene aggressively with the goal to prolong life, no matter what cost. This option would include inserting a feeding tube tomorrow, consideration of dialysis if her kidneys could not keep up with her fluids, and even intubation with a respirator if her breathing got worse.

Anita spoke up and announced the ground rules for their discussion. "Everyone has an opportunity to speak tonight. However, when someone is speaking, please do not interrupt. Let them say their peace."

They started on Dr. Smith's left side and took turns going around the circle. Some family members were eloquent, others disjointed but impassioned. At Miles turn, he presented his position like an attorney, arguing a case before a jury. Many family members abstained from sharing an opinion. Dr. Smith listened intently, looking at the clock from time to time, wondering how all of these people would come to a consensus tonight. She had sat through many a family meeting, but never one so large, and never with such polarized opinions.

Forty-five minutes had passed when Anita's turn came. Anita channeled the authority of being a minister and spoke to the room as she might her congregation. "Brothers and Sisters, we are at a crisis point for our family. I have watched our behaviors deteriorate over the last 24 hours. It is entirely uncalled for. We are family!" Anita paused, and several said Amen. "I have thought long and hard about what we should do tonight." The room silenced as the family hung on each word Anita said. "It is clear to me, that to survive as a family, which Mimi desired most of all, we need to have a vote."

Dr. Smith's eyebrows arched, clearly, she was not expecting this. Several other family members also looked confused. Anita clarified, "I am going to hand out pieces of paper and pens, and each person in this room is going to vote on what we should do. This will be a secret ballot, so that we won't hold grudges with each other in the future."

Slight murmurs of conversation began as Anita reached under her chair to a bag from the hospital gift shop. She began to pass out pens labeled University of Kansas Hospital and copier paper ripped in half. Junior spoke up, "Nita, what exactly should we write on this paper?"

While Anita paused to think, Anthony cut in, "It's quite simple, write either the word live or die." Unperturbed with this response, family members hovered over their papers, some quickly scribbling their response, others biting their pens, having not made up their minds yet.

Dr. Smith sat taking it all in. She thought about Mimi lying in her hospital bed not 10 feet from the conference room. She had no qualms having her own opinion that Mimi was trying to die. She was mentally gone, no longer able to eat, walk, or communicate. She was essentially a body, a soul trapped. What would Mimi say to all of this?

Anita's voice interrupted Dr. Smith's contemplation. "Dr. Smith, if you don't mind, we'd like you to count the votes." She handed over a large stack of folded papers. Dr. Smith's stomach tightened, she was not sure she wanted to take part in this unusual affair. Anita, sensing Dr. Smith's hesitancy said with desperation, "Please."

Dr. Smith nodded, rising and accepting the papers. "I'll just step out to count them," she said, not wanting the others to watch her as she counted votes. Unexpectedly, her hand trembled slightly as she turned to the nurse's station. Thankfully, the nurses and aides were busy with other patients and ignored her. She decided she would separate out the results and then count them if necessary. Methodically she opened each paper. *Die, Live, Live, Die.* Dr. Smith took a breath and emotionally distanced herself from the situation as she continued to count.

As soon as she finished, she tossed the papers into the shredder bin on her way back to the conference room, the closeness of the vote surprised her. The friction in the room as she entered was palpable. The way all eyes turned towards her with anticipation reminded her of the looks families give surgeons when the surgeon steps out of the operating room with information.

Dr. Smith purposefully inhaled very slowly. "We will place the feeding tube tomorrow morning." Someone yelled, "Yes!"

with enthusiasm usually reserved for points scored from a favorite sports team. Dr. Smith did not have the stomach to stay and searched out Anita's face before she left. Anita's face sagged with grief, the look in her eyes was that of despair. The wall of disassociation Dr. Smith had put up began to dissolve, and she quickly left the room, a tear escaping down one cheek.

She popped into Mimi's room on her way out, sensing she only had moments before the family would drift in. It was dusk outside and with no lights on in the room, it was eerily dark. Mimi was utterly unchanged. The sound of oxygen blowing through her mask was the only noise in the room.

15. WALLS

Audrey

Abeeping sound sifted into Audrey's subconscious as she slept. At first it played in the periphery of her dream, then suddenly it stung her awareness; it was her pager. At once she was awake, silencing the black box before it woke her two-year-old daughter in the next room. The neon aqua number displayed was the Hospice House, and she grabbed her cell phone coaxing her brain to be sharp.

She cleared her throat to shake the sleep from her voice, "This is Doctor Clark, someone paged." She felt her husband, Derek, shift next to her, and realized she should lower her voice.

"This is Tom, sorry to wake you."

"No, it's fine, what is it?" Audrey felt her heart quicken. Despite being a Hospice Physician for several years, she still feared that she wouldn't be able to solve whatever problem one of the nurses paged her about.

"I just wanted to let you know that Terrence in room 14 passed away at 2:35 A.M."

Audrey's pulse immediately slowed, there would be no challenging crisis to solve, and this death had been expected. "I assume it was peaceful? Anything I should know?"

"Yes, very peaceful," Tim explained, "We had just repositioned him. His family was in the room sleeping, and then his daughter woke up to sudden silence and came and got me."

"Okay. Thanks for letting me know." Audrey ended the call and was just about to lay back down when she heard her daughter, Izzy, whimpering in the next room. Since she was already awake, she decided to go check on her.

Audrey peered over the railings of the crib to see Izzy curled up in a tight ball, chubby arms wrapped around her chubby legs. "Ah, you're cold!" Audrey whispered, finding the blanket and tucking it around Izzy.

A yawn bubbled up the back of Audrey's throat, reminding her it was time to get back to sleep. Easing back into bed she silently wished for no more pages and that slumber would take her quickly, despite knowing how unlikely those two scenarios were.

Audrey pulled her Jeep Grand Cherokee into the rear parking lot at the Kansas City Hospice House, the forty-minute commute settling into her neck muscles as tension. Before exiting, Audrey reached her right hand back to knead the tight muscles of her trapezius. She winced at the tender knots which were the physical evidence of the stress she carried from taking care of dying patients for a living.

Mentally she readied herself for another day as she walked the short steps to the rear employee entrance. The path to her office took her down the large main C- shaped hallway which was lined with patient rooms on one side and large floor to ceiling windows facing the private gardens of the Hospice House on the other.

She registered that something was different. Her brisk pace slowed, and she turned her attention solely outdoors. She could see across the gardens to the other wing of the Hospice House, and her eyes scanned from that distance towards her own position, trying to decipher what was different. It was the middle of October, and her vision took in the ochre and rust colored leaves both on the trees and scattered on the ground. The early freeze two weeks prior had cleared the garden of flowers. However, as Audrey's gaze focused on the mulched beds nearest to the glass windowpane, her eyes widened; planted in the mulch and in large pots of soil on this side of the garden were bunches of fake plastic flowers. The cacophony of color, unseasonal to fall, assaulted her senses.

"Aren't they beautiful?" Victoria, a nurse at the Hospice House, had slipped, unnoticed, next to Audrey, startling her.

Audrey wasn't sure what answer to give, as bright colored plastic flowers weren't what she had expected. "They are certainly unique and cheery." Audrey turned to Victoria inquisitively, hoping for a story.

Victoria's eyes twinkled and her entire face seemed to be grinning. "They're from Room 10." Audrey concentrated, shuffling through the Rolodex of patients in her brain, landing on Ben, an eight-year-old boy who was dying from a brain tumor.

Audrey looked perplexed, so Victoria continued, her amusement growing, "He was out in his wheel chair yesterday and met Mrs. Carlson from Room 11. Mrs. Carlson's family had pushed her bed out of the room for her to view our gardens. She was a Master Gardner, I'm told." Victoria kept going, "Ben was out near Mrs. Carlson and overheard her lamenting that she would not be alive this year to enjoy spring and how the bright flowers were always her favorite."

Victoria concluded her story with glistening eyes, "Ben whispered to his mom and dad, 'We should get some flowers for her, it would make her so happy.' What parent can turn down such a request? Ben and his parents recruited some of the other families here yesterday afternoon to help and got them all planted."

Audrey was washed in warmth at the kindness of Ben's idea. She looked again at the fake flowers scattered in nearby pots and in the beds outside the windows, their gaudiness instantly transformed to beauty.

"By the way, Dr. Clark, Ben's mom did want to talk to you about increasing his steroid. He's stopped eating again and is back to being drowsy like he was two weeks ago."

Audrey sighed, coming back to the reality of her job. "Okay, thanks. I'll start with her after I run my things to my desk and collect myself." Mentally it had been tough taking care of Ben. She noticed each day it took more effort to protect herself from experiencing Ben's decline personally as a mother.

Audrey's office consisted of a cubicle in a room shared with Hospice social workers, chaplains, and volunteers. At her cubicle Audrey noted a medical chart and death certificate. She scrunched up her nose, knowing she'd need to take care of that before starting rounds. She got her laptop plugged in and turned on, then took the file in her hands.

The death certificate was already filled out with all of the demographic information, including the name Kyanna typed in small font at the top. It was the middle section labeled "Cause of Death" that Audrey was responsible for. A blank line with the words "Due to (or as a consequence of):" stared at her. She knew that this patient, Kyanna, had died of Metastatic Renal Cell Cancer and wrote that in the box, but had to sift through the chart to recall when she had been diagnosed. She found the dates she was looking for, and mentally calculated the time frame, writing '2 Years' into the box labeled "Approximate interval between onset and death."

When she got to the section about the time of death, she paused briefly, recalling what a unique and unnerving death Kyanna had. Her actual death, the instant her heart ceased beating and her breathing stopped, had been but a wisp of a moment, a thread that had finally snapped. But the process itself, had taken nearly a month. Audrey had never seen someone fight death as much as Kyanna. She lamented internally that there was nowhere on the death certificate to mention this.

Audrey finished the death certificate and knew it was time to tackle visiting Ben, so she grabbed her stethoscope from her satchel and placed it around her neck and headed to Room 10.

Ben's hospice room had taken on the look of a boy's room. Large stuffed dinosaurs, an Avenger's poster, and sugary snacks littered the space. Ben was in bed, bald head and overly round chubby features from the chronic steroids. Audrey was glad for the visual changes, as it made it easier to separate Ben from other eight-year-olds she knew. Ben was asleep, and his mother, Michelle, quickly strode over to Audrey, ready for a discussion. After nearly 16 days at the Hospice House, formalities were absent, and Audrey and Michelle jumped right into the concern.

"Did Victoria tell you about the changes?" Michelle asked her voice thick with concern.

"She did. Did it happen suddenly, or have you noticed him getting weaker and sleeping more over a few days?"

Michelle thought for a moment, "I suppose a few days. I just was hoping it wasn't a real setback. He's like he was when we came in here. It's just so hard to watch. Can we go up on the steroids again?"

Audrey had increased Ben's dexamethasone when he first was admitted, and the improvement had been dramatic. Ben's lethargy and unwillingness to eat had vanished. "It's a good question and for this decision, there is no correct answer. As you have seen, steroids only have a limited boost effect. It's usually around 2 weeks. I would guess if we doubled his dexamethasone, you'd see the same improvement as you did when you came in."

Michelle's face was receptive and encouraged, she opened her mouth to say let's do it, when Audrey continued, "Here's the problem. This is the last jump we can make. After this increase, when he starts to decline… that's it. I can't just give more steroids then." Michelle's expression immediately clouded. Audrey could tell she was weighing the decision. Both women looked over at Ben.

Audrey opened herself up, wondering what she would do in this situation. Instantly, feelings of dread and grief swelled inside, and she saw her two-year-old daughter, Izzy, in the bed. Tears welled and Audrey felt she would soon be engulfed with sorrow. Fearing she would be unable to surface if she allowed herself even another instant of empathy, she ratcheted the emotional door shut with a blink and turned her entire body away from Ben. Michelle still gazed at her son, half of her lip caught in her teeth.

Michelle finally spoke, stuttering, "I, I think... you know, I'm going to need to run this one by my husband." As an after-thought she added, "And maybe I can see if Ben has anything to say about it."

Most of Audrey's mental energy was still being used to keep herself detached, but she was able to nod in confirmation and found a way to finish her visit without any further close calls.

Outside the room she didn't even pause to collect her thoughts, but barreled into the next room, purposefully avoiding a glance towards the panes of glass facing the gardens.

The next several patients were more standard cases. Older individuals, who had lived full lives, had supportive families, and little complications.

In no time, Audrey found herself before Room 15, which be-longed to Mikki.   Mikki was a few years younger than Audrey. She and her husband, Ty, had been married only four years. They had been High School sweethearts, dated through college, and after a year of marriage Mikki was diagnosed with Melanoma.

Audrey guessed the room would be full. Mikki had made her transition to active dying the afternoon before and Audrey had spent over an hour walking the family through the process of what was coming. She was no longer conscious, and the extend-ed family had all been called in. Wondering what state the room would be in, Audrey slowly eased open the door, peaking her head into the space.

The mood was somber and expectant.   The chairs huddled around the bed held Mikki's parents, grandparents, and older siblings. Ty was in bed with Mikki, stretched out on her right side; his right hand clutched her left hand as it rested across her chest. Mikki was ghostly white and her lips held a bluish hue. Her breathing was shallow and quick. Audrey realized a few of the family members were singing softly together. As Audrey stepped further into the room, she recognized an old church hymn.

A few of the family glanced at Audrey and then immediately focused back on Mikki. Mikki's mother, Sue, however, kept her gaze at Audrey, inviting conversation. Audrey stepped softly to Sue who had been seated at the head of the bed to Mikki's left. Audrey gently placed her hand on Sue's back in sympathy and whispered, "She looks comfortable."

Sue nodded and spoke, "We're just waiting now."

Audrey guessed she'd be back in later and didn't want to intrude. "We don't need to make any changes, so I'll let you have your privacy." Audrey's voice was hushed and added, "But let us know if you need anything." Audrey glanced over at Ty, trying to assess his mental state. He looked only at his dying wife and seemed oblivious of Audrey's presence.

Back outside in the hallway, a hunger pain made Audrey glance at her watch; 11:45 A.M. She was miffed that she was still making rounds this late in the morning. Just then, Victoria came buzzing by, clearly on a mission. She threw out words to Audrey as she passed, "New one just pulled up."

Audrey was caught off guard, "What new one?" she questioned.

By now Victoria was nearly out of site, on her way to meet the ambulance at the back door. Her response was faint, "Room 17. Transfer from Providence."

Audrey's jaw clenched. She hadn't heard of a new admit and hated being behind the ball. Without much choice, she went to hunt down paper work on the new patient, so as not to appear foolish when she met them. She found the stack of papers, which had been faxed from the hospital, at the nurse's station. She shuffled through insurance information and demographics to find the jewel; the History and Physical form.

The H and P always provided the quickest summary, and Audrey skimmed the words, forming a picture of who had just arrived. Bert Hamm was a 78-year-old man who had fallen in his garage, was taken to the hospital and found to have had a massive stroke. He was widowed and had two sons; Foster and Parker.

The hospital had treated things aggressively, but after 72 hours it was clear that Bert would not be waking up. His children had decided to support previous discussions they'd had with him and allow a natural death from the stroke. Audrey jumped several more pages, searching for medications and nurses notes from the last day. She was relieved to see they hadn't been pumping him full of intravenous fluids, which at times ended up prolonging the dying process.

There was commotion to Audrey's left as the Emergency Medical Technicians rolled a stretcher past Audrey. Victoria and T'Neek, one of the aides, accompanied them. This first look at the patient always told Audrey helpful information. Sometimes patients came in talking, sometimes combative and disoriented. Bert however was unresponsive, and Audrey noticed his breathing was exaggerated and agonal in nature. She locked eyes with Victoria, and both understood each other's thoughts; Bert would only be with them a very short time.

The medical entourage turned and entered Room 17. Audrey moved to follow, hoping to see family close behind. After a moment, seeing no one, she decided to head in to see Bert. She entered the room, hovering on the periphery of the action. The team was transferring Bert to the bed. Two were on the stretcher side and two reached their arms across the hospice bed. They took hold of a thick pad underneath Bert and someone called out "On three. One, Two and Three." With a grunt, Bert's body was hoisted and heaved onto the bed. The EMTs gathered their supplies while Victoria and T'Neek stripped Bert of his hospital gown to hand back to the transport team and replace it with a new one. Once unclothed, Audrey was alarmed to see progressive dark bluish mottling in a patchwork up both of his legs and thighs, and she noted his feet were a solid deep purple color, indicating an advanced dying process.

Both crews worked in prescribed rituals that Audrey silently observed. She interrupted the EMTs to ask, "Do you know if the family was following?"

"Should be just a few minutes behind us," the EMT answered chuckling. "We were speeding a bit, I wasn't sure we would make it here before he died! Lu couldn't even get a pressure on him our last ten minutes." Both EMT's acknowledged their precarious transport with knowing looks.

There was a knock on the door and Audrey turned hoping to see family. Instead, one of the other hospice aides, Jane, poked her head in. "Sorry to interrupt, but Dr. Clark, we need you in Room 15."

Audrey knew from Jane's countenance that Mikki must have just passed and sucked in an audible breath through her teeth. She looked over at Victoria apologetically and offered, "I'll write orders after this, but if he needs any morphine for breathing, consider this a verbal for 5 to 10mg every hour as needed."

Victoria looked up from her assessment and nodded, then Audrey added, "If you need me in here, send Jane to grab me."

Jane walked with Audrey back to Room 15, confirming as they walked that Mikki had just passed. Audrey braced herself for the mourning family, trying to let the concern over Bert's imminent death without family present, float away. In the same fashion as she had earlier, Audrey eased open the door. The view was nearly identical, except the family was all standing around the bed, rather than sitting. Audrey was relieved to see the Hospice chaplain, Jim, already in the room, his arms in a loose embrace with Mikki's Mom and Dad.

Jim looked toward Audrey and invited her into the circle with his expression. In his mellow and comforting voice, he said, "We were just getting ready to have a prayer." Audrey assented and found a spot in the circle at the foot of the bed between the grandparents and a sibling. She noticed Ty was curled up in bed still, hand cupping the side of Mikki's frozen face. He stared at her with an intensity that reminded Audrey of the way new mothers take in every detail of their newborns. Jim's soothing prayer began, and Audrey let her eyes close. The stillness began to chip at Audrey's firm walls, and she felt the situational reality settle on her. The grief in the room nuzzled its way into her and tears began to form.

As Jim's prayer concluded a sudden loud moan started. Audrey's eyes flew open to find the source. The moan came from Ty, and quickly escalated to a panicked scream as he began to yell, "She's not breathing.... She's not breathing!" Ty's eyes were saucer wide and his stare drilled holes into Mikki's half open mouth.

It had been at least 15 minutes since Mikki had breathed her last, but reality was just sinking in for Ty. The sincerity of his shock caused an emotional eruption in the room. Ty's brother knelt and gave him a bear hug from behind and whispered, "Let her go," as tears streamed from his face. Ty, however, was in a trance, an emotional seizure of sorts. He fought his brother's hold and dove into his wife's body saying, "Once more, let me hold you one more time."

Something cracked inside Audrey and a well of tears flooded

her eyes. The partition of detachment, so carefully constructed, had been blown apart. Audrey stepped backwards, away from the circle and found herself wondering what a last embrace with someone you love must be like. Her hands covered her face trying to hide the emotion from anyone daring to look away from Ty's last hug with his wife.

She needed to get out of that room, and she knew she needed some time to collect herself. She attempted to contain her sadness temporarily, until she could reach a safe place. She wiped the overt tears on her sleeve and stepped out of the room. She moved to make her way to her office and heard her name being called. She had a hard time processing who was calling, as every fiber beckoned her to escape to her cubicle so she could cry in private.

"Dr. Clark," the bid came again. Audrey forced herself to turn towards the voice. It was Victoria, who immediately saw the marks of tears and blotchiness on Audrey's face. "I'm sorry," she said self-consciously, "but Room 17's family got here and…" She made a face of dismay, "he passed just now."

"You're not serious, are you?"

Victoria scrunched up her nose apologetically, "I am, and they really want to see you."

Audrey felt a buzzing in her head as she forced the images of Mikki and Ty down into herself. She searched for anything genuine to offer the strangers in Room 17 and came up empty. But at the same time, she knew she had a job to do. She pressed her fingertips into her forehead and pulled the skin taught, trying to force the sorrow back into her brain. She already looked grief stricken, so needed no adjustment to her expression. She walked a few steps to Bert's room in a stodgy way, her body protesting.

It was not ideal to meet someone for the first time at the bedside of their deceased relative, and Audrey heaved a sigh and gingerly opened the door. The scene was eerily similar to the room she had just exited. Family stood around the bedside mournfully, though this time a large elderly man lay with mouth half opened, face fixed.

Awkwardly Audrey approached the family with a regretful look. She lowered her voice as they all turned her direction, "Hi. I'm Dr. Clark. I am so sorry I didn't have a chance to greet you earlier." She quickly read their expressions for any disappointment or displeasure and saw none. She continued, "He went so quickly. I am just glad you all made it."

Those in the room nodded, eyes moist all around. A younger version of Bert stepped to shake Audrey's hand, adding, "We are just happy he made it here. This place is so beautiful and peaceful. He deserved this."

Audrey could feel them scrutinize the signs of grief on her face, and they warmed instantly to her. A woman came and reached to give Audrey a hug, "Thank you for everything you did for him, even though he wasn't here long. He didn't suffer at all."

Audrey guessed that they assumed her sadness was for them, a gift, sympathizing with their own grief. She felt like an imposter, and longed to flee the room. In truth, she was still in Room 15.

"Well, I just wanted to give my condolences," Audrey said with a mock mournful smile, "take your time and let us know if you need anything." The family members continued to wipe their eyes and drew their attention back to Bert allowing Audrey to slip out.

Straight across from Room 17 was the counter to the Nurses Station, and Audrey immediately walked to it, supporting her elbow on the high surface and allowing her head to rest fully in her hand. There were remnants of the sorrow from earlier still simmering, but the disingenuous encounter had buffered much of the emotion. In its place, she found exhaustion.

"Two in less than an hour," Victoria's familiar voice was fatigued as well. The two shared a look of incredulousness.

Audrey glanced at her watch, "How is it nearly two o'clock? I think I'm going to go eat something." Inwardly, Audrey wanted a break to process the last hour. She felt her insides being ripped with incongruent feelings, part of her authentically sad and part of her numb from the routine of death.

"Before you do, can you just stop into Ben's Room. I think they've made a decision on what to do."

Audrey nodded wearily, consciously burying the idea that she'd have time to sort out her feelings. Time warped in a strange way, making the earlier encounter with Ben and his mom seem like a different day. Audrey tipped her head towards Victoria as she left the Nurses station, wondering what the decision for Ben would be.

As she walked past Mikki's Room, she felt a lurch deep inside and imagined a large hand pushing downward and sealing her wisps of lament. Another time, she thought. At Ben's room, she found Michelle just getting ready to enter with a plate full of fresh baked chocolate chip cookies. Audrey's stomach rumbled as they greeted each other. Michelle commented as they entered the room, "You all spoil us around here with all these fresh baked goods!"

"We love our volunteers, that's for sure!" Audrey quipped.

Inside the room Ben was awake, sitting up in bed, and watching a Disney movie. He smiled at Audrey, his round cheeks puckering. Audrey teased Ben, "I'm surprised to see you awake, you were snoring this morning."

Michelle found the remote and muted the movie and answered, "I know. I was shocked, too. But it allowed us to have a good talk, right Benny?"

Ben nodded at his Mom but kept his eyes on the movie still playing soundlessly. Michelle and Audrey stood on opposite sides of the bed and Michelle naturally rubbed Ben's bald head as she spoke. "We talked about how nice it's been these two weeks, especially for John and me, our family, and Ben's friends."

Michelle looked at her son and Audrey noticed tears forming in the rims of Michelle's eye lids. She braced herself for what would come next. Michelle continued, "Ben let his Dad and I know that he was tired," Michelle swallowed hard, fighting more tears. She took a deep breath, "He's ready to be done."

Michelle raised her gaze to Audrey, who saw the anguish present in Michelle's eyes. Audrey thought she'd try to confirm this, and rested her hand on Ben's forearm, drawing his attention away from the movie. "So, no more meds, huh, Ben?"

Ben nodded in agreement. Though his speech was a bit garbled Audrey clearly heard his next words, "I'm not afraid." He focused back to his movie as Michelle wiped tears from her eyes. Audrey knew better than to open the door to the emotional implications of this decision and kept her countenance strictly informative.

"What now?" Michelle asked, leaving Ben's side to discuss things more privately with Audrey.

"Not much will change. That grogginess he had this morning will become more pronounced. He'll sleep more and more and probably have a harder time communicating. If he's hungry and can eat, let him, though I would guess that will get less and less."

Michelle took it all in, still wrestling with her tears. "And time?" she asked.

Audrey mentally thought through the things that effected prognosis, adding and subtracting days based on patterns she'd observed in the past. "I'm going to guess one week at the shortest, up to three weeks at the longer end." Despite having asked the question and wanting actual numbers, Michelle choked back a sob.

"I'm sorry," Audrey said reacting to the response, feeling herself on the brink again of losing it.

Michelle put up one hand to block the apology, using her other hand to cover her mouth. "It's okay, I needed to know. I just…. It's just…" She shook her head finding no words to convey what she was feeling.

Audrey wanted to reach out and embrace Michelle but knew it would cause the last barrier holding the tide of heartbreak back, to collapse. Instead she offered a final look of compassion and exited the room.

On auto-pilot Audrey made her way back to her cubicle desk and crumpled into her chair. She reached for the computer, hitting the enter key to wake it up and noticed someone had left two chocolate chip cookies for her. Gratitude washed over her, and she snatched one, contemplating savoring each bite. Her will power faded rapidly with the first taste, and in seconds both cookies had been engulfed.

The small clock on the lower right hand of her computer screen reminded her the day was nearly done. She needed to leave by 4:45 P.M. at the latest to make it to Izzy's daycare in time to pick her up. She quickly did the math, calculating she had almost two hours to get all her documentation done from the day. Her nose wrinkled unconsciously, two hours would not be enough, which meant she would be sitting on her couch after Izzy went to bed apathetically finishing her notes.

Audrey gave herself a pep talk as she opened the Electronic Medical Record and scrolled to the patient list. The challenge was to take the day's conversations, observations, data, and exams and narrate a picture for the benefit of insurance companies. When she got to the last note that she had time for, she paused, seeing Mikki's name. Her mind replayed the scene from earlier in the day. In the empty box labeled "Subjective" Audrey typed:

Reason for visit:
Follow up of 31 y.o. female with metastatic melanoma that transitioned to active dying yesterday. Follow up pain and dyspnea. Family support.
First visit this morning, patient in bed, unresponsive, no signs of distress. Family at bedside anticipating immanent death. Medications given as needed for signs of pain and dyspnea, overall trend down in past 24 hours.
Second visit made at time of passing. Family grieving appropriately, support given. Time of death 12:07 P.M.

Audrey went on to write the details of the objective or physical part of the note, adding in some lines of assessment. She felt a resurgence of the nagging contrast inwardly of the hollow written words and the reality of a husband's last moments with his wife. She didn't know what to do with the experience of being a witness to that event, and so she hit the save button, exited the program, closed her lap top, and tucked it in her satchel next to her uneaten lunch.

On the drive home, Audrey's husband, Derek called to say he had finished clinic early and would pick up Izzy. She felt some of the pressure of rush hour traffic melt away knowing she didn't need to worry about being late. She let the lull of the voices on the radio updating the news, wash over her. She let her car take her away from her day, from her work, from the deaths, and from the emotions.

When she pulled in her driveway, she was sure she had reinforced her walls separating work from her family. She stepped out of her Jeep, eager for the comfort of home. But then it happened; Audrey saw the round chubby face of her daughter at the glassed screen door. Izzy had her hands and face smashed into the glass, her bald head with only wisps of light blond hair reminded her of Ben. Derek opened the door behind Izzy, allowing her to stumble outside, grinning and shouting, "Momma!" with glee.

Audrey stooped to sweep her daughter into her arms. As she pressed Izzy's squishy little body into her own, she thought of Michelle and Ben, Ty and Mikki. Down came the bolstered block of compartmentalization and Audrey began to weep. She wanted to hold Izzy indefinitely, but felt her squirm in the locked embrace. She loosened her grip reluctantly and Izzy searched her mother's face.

"Why sad, Momma?" Izzy looked concerned and a bit frightened.

Audrey glanced up at Derek, who too, looked alarmed. She felt the tears dripping from her eyes. She knew, though the temptation was to give way to the fear of losing them, that she had to turn this around quickly. She compressed the sorrow inside of her, forcing it smaller and smaller, until it transformed itself into gratitude. She looked back at Izzy and pulled her in for another hug, less desperate this time, and answered, "I'm just so happy and so lucky to have you."

AUTHOR'S NOTE

My hope in writing this fictional collection of stories was to transport you, dear reader, into a unique and hallowed space. Perhaps you have walked this end of life journey with someone. If so, you know how complicated and sacred it is; the discord and the peace that are present. In the midst of the physical process of dying there lies an opportunity to learn about living. This is what these stories are meant to convey.

While the details and back stories and characters themselves are complete fiction, each of these stories are based on experiences I had as a Palliative Care doctor. I ended many of my workdays thinking how the truth is often more vivid and extreme than all the fiction we try to create.

The field of Hospice and Palliative Medicine is a gift to society. To those of you who work or have ever worked in this amazing profession I say Thank you!

I must also express my gratitude for the women who read my drafts and corrected my errors- Erin, Linda, and Tami, you were a godsend! And of course my biggest fan- Cre'. Thank you to my friends and family who pushed and encouraged me to write, despite my natural inertia.

Made in the USA
Monee, IL
26 March 2021

63887739R00135